The Wall People

AnneMarie Dapp

I0571534

For Mom

Acknowledgements

I would like to thank my friends and family for their support during the making of this novel. My husband, Dale, and our children, Eric and Lindsay, were constant pillars of inspiration. I am forever grateful for my best friends, Darci and Maria, for showing me the face of true friendship. Thank you, Steven and David Rockwell, for your belief in your little sister. There were so many wonderful people that helped me along the way. Your names could easily fill an entire book. Lastly, I want to thank our Heavenly Father for his guidance and strength during this beautiful journey. God Bless.

AnneMarie Dapp
August 28, 2015

Let us go forth, the tellers of tales,
And seize whatever prey the heart longs for,
And have no fear.
Everything exists,
Everything is true,
And the earth is only
A little dust
Under our feet.
W.B Yeats "The Celtic Twilight"

Prologue

Her heart raced in her chest. The heavy gown dragged and snagged the ground with each painful step. The sharp cries of ravens echoed in the distance, their shrill voices lamenting the approaching twilight. Jagged stones protruded along the trail. Her bare feet suffered painfully from the brutal terrain. Rich soil began to take on a sandy texture as she neared the shoreline. Daylight faded and washed shadows over the lush landscape. If she could only find her way back to the safety of the main road, back to the village of Kinvara. The aroma of the sea was rich, intoxicating. Woodlands quickly gave way to an open shore. Dark waters raged and heaved against the rising tide. Rock cliffs on both sides surrounded her. She had followed the wrong path.

The icy water rolled toward her as she slowed at the sandy bank. With resignation, she watched the churning waves of Galway Bay. Dunguaire Castle appeared like a phantom beacon on the foggy haze. Dim lights glowed in the windows of the grand building. Cold ripples drifted over her battered feet. The water was salty and harsh on her open wounds. Taking a deep breath, embracing the pain, she made the sign of the cross and whispered a silent prayer to Jesus and the Mother Mary. Heavy footsteps made their way toward her. Inhaling the aroma of the overlapping waves calmed her mind. He stood directly behind her in silence. The young woman held her ground. Rough hands encircled her delicate neck. Her locket ripped from her throat as she was pulled under the frigid water. It floated away on the currents. Her last thoughts were of Daniel.

CHAPTER 1

Katie awoke with a jolt. The radio alarm sprang into action with Rhianna's plaintive vocals. Its digital numbers clicked to reveal the hour of 4:30am. Darkness and fog drifted outside her window. Florescent lights flickered from the street below. It was a typically cold San Francisco morning. Leaving her warm bed, the sound of her feet echoed down the hallway on their way to turn up the thermostat. Half awake, she made her way into the kitchen and found a recycled paper cup. Within a few minutes, the whistle shrieked its welcoming call. She stirred in an extra spoonful of the instant coffee and added a generous portion of sugar. As her drowsiness faded, the reality of the day became apparent. The excitement of new opportunities eclipsed the anxiety of the work ahead. For the next few hours, she gathered her remaining possessions. Box after box was methodically removed from the cubicle-sized residence. When the last of her supplies were finally carried out, she took one last look and closed the door. The apartment key was placed carefully inside a small envelope and slipped quietly under the manager's mat. The job was over, a weight lifted.

She walked the length of the corridor leading to the dark garage. The blue jeep was completely full. The old car was half her age and still going strong. The back of the vehicle was piled high with boxes and clothes. Sliding into the driver's seat, she quickly noticed her reflection in the rear view mirror. Her bright green eyes radiated the promise of new beginnings.

Life had worn her down over the years. Perhaps it had started with the men in her life. If only you could erase the past. A romantic at heart, she would soon learn that relationships do not always end well.

Her marriage of ten years had ended bitterly. She'd discovered that words had the power to puncture one's soul. Not to say that she had never felt the back of her husband's hand. Jake had a mean way to him after a few drinks. But it was the words she could not let go of. They echoed in her mind, painful and cruel, each driving its own special agony. Her self-esteem and confidence had been slowly chipped way. Now, at age forty, she searched for traces of herself.

As she exits the apartment complex, she is struck by the beauty of the morning. The brisk air drifts from open vents on the driver's side. She breathes in the fresh breeze mingled with a distant scent of chimney smoke. Fall is beginning to stake its claim in Northern California. The morning sky stirs brightly with scarlet streaks. The Golden Gate Bridge waits in all of its industrial glory. The unforgettable jewel, beckoning the dreamers of the world to celebrate and become one with her beautiful city.

Katie is always struck by a sense of nostalgic loss when leaving. The Bay is magnificent, subtle in its simplicity. The Pacific waters churn and cascade in orchestrated rhythm. A thousand little boats dance and play on its tides. The fog slowly burns away to reveal the glorious cityscape, the skyline reminding her of an old saying:

Red sky at night, sailors delight.

Red sky at morning, sailors take warning;

The image reminds her of her family. The O'Brien's were seventh generation Irish immigrants. Stories of the old country had been passed down from mother to daughter over the decades. Magical tales of the emerald isle had always intrigued her and left her with a sense of nostalgia. As a young woman, Katie had found it laughable that her mother considered the history of the Potato Famine, or as she called it, The Great Hunger, a personally upsetting experience. But as she grew older, the stories of the past resonated more deeply for her.

At times it seemed as if her Irish ancestors were whispering to her from the shadows. She never shunned an opportunity to pick up a nice book on the subject. She was particularly fascinated by the way the Celtic people seemed to embody great humor while falling prey to their darkest depression. She found it best summed up by Yeats. In describing a character, he wrote "Being Irish, he had an abiding sense of tragedy; which sustained him through temporary periods of joy."

The same could be said of her personality. It was too easy to become lost in the injustices of the world and the cruel circumstances of the innocent. She often had trouble sleeping after watching the evening news. Images of violence and horrific crimes troubled her mind and heart. Sometimes it was too much.

The day opened up before her. Late morning found her craving a warm breakfast and the opportunity to stretch her legs. With a little patience she would be home in a few hours. What do you do with a dream materialized? She would soon learn.

CHAPTER 2

The jeep was headed to Napa Valley. The region is known for its rolling hills, lush vineyards, and lavish living. For Katie, the Valley conjured images of paintings hanging in quaint bed and breakfasts. These artworks always possessed a similar composition. The canvases displayed quiet country cottages surrounded by vineyards. Interestingly, the scenes often suggested the late afternoon sun. As car after car rolled by, she began to fantasize about her new life as if it were a work of art. The image of an unfinished painting surfaced in her mind.

A little cottage off in the distance. It would not take long to reach this residence. The path was bordered with strawberry plants. The air was warm and smelled faintly of honeysuckle. The home came closer into view with each footstep. She climbed the weak stairs one by one. Her hand on the cold ceramic doorknob, she twists and the door is already ajar. She gives the wooden barrier a gentle push and is suddenly met with the shriek of squealing, rubber tires and the deadly blare of a car horn's maddening wail.

In her daydreams, the jeep veers dangerously close to the dividing line on the country road. This small lapse in judgment had almost brought her into a head-on collision with a silver Porsche. The glint of the car's passenger mirror caught the glare of an elderly man. *My God*, she thought to herself. *What are you doing?* This was not the first time she'd lost track of time. Nor would it be the last.

Her heart pounding in her ears, she pulled the car to the side of the road. Reality poured over her like cold rain. After several minutes, her pulse regained its normal rhythm. A strand of cold sweat trickled down the small of her back. She was startled to realize how much time had passed. Her low blood sugar threatened to undermine her. Her empty stomach protested with a faint rumble. She had to find a place to eat and to regain her bearings.

Katie turned the key in the ignition and shifted her car into neutral. The grinding of metal jarred her senses. *Great*, she thought. The clutch was out again. She followed the exit into the town of Petaluma. Main Street was lined with modest cafés and bookstores. If she were not in such a hurry, she would spend the afternoon hunting for books in the quaint shops. Katie loved to have a nice stock on hand when the winter rains began. After a couple blocks, a café called "Grandma's Cookie Jar" caught her eye.

She found a parking spot in the far corner of the front entrance. Eagerly driving over, she realized that an old Ford pickup had taken up half the space. It took three tries before her jeep would fit into the spot. "Nice." She slipped out from the driver's side and squeezed between the two vehicles. She noticed the peeling primer from the truck. A tattered Confederate flag was tied to its cab bed. Entering the café, she was greeted by the familiar aroma of espresso beans and warm baked bread. The specials were written on a black board by the front counter. Someone had added their own personal touch to the illustrations. The details appeared professional.

An assortment of tempting pastries lined the display cases. Two large flies hovered over the desserts. A woman in her early twenties absently wiped down the counters. The server appeared annoyed when asked about the specials. Katie asked if their eggs came from cage-free chickens. The idea of chickens confined in cramped cages was simply barbaric. Satisfied with her answer, Katie ordered an egg salad croissant and a soy latte. As the girl prepared the order, she took in the place.

The café had a country farm theme. There were several paintings of baked apple pies and scenes of whimsical livestock. The tables sported red and white checkered tablecloths. A frail, elderly woman at the front counter appeared mesmerized by her plate of waffles. Syrup dripped lazily down her mouth and chin. Katie quickly looked away. As she placed her order, she noticed a sleeve of tattoos on the girl behind the counter. The ink depicted a dark and moody forest. The bright eyes of the wild animals gazed through the tangled woods. It was remarkable. She looked up at the young woman's face. Her jet-black hair was cropped haphazardly. Two gauges matched the silver stud in her nose. It had been many years since Katie had lived the life of a rebellious art student, since she'd dyed her hair every color under the sun. These youthful memories seemed too far away.

Katie paid for her lunch and found a quiet table in the back. A painting of dancing pigs hung above her chair. She took a bite of her croissant and experienced the unpleasant sensation of biting into a broken eggshell. It felt like nails on a chalkboard. It was a subtle reminder that a vegan diet might be more suited to her tastes. Her mind drifted to all of the work ahead. It was going to be a long afternoon. Movers would be arriving in a few hours. They would be bringing her furniture to her new home. She tried to relax and finish the rest of her meal. A little silver bell jingled over the front door. Two young men entered the café. The wind played with the curtains behind them. They were dressed in work jeans and tight fitting t-shirts. Their clothes were covered in dried mud. The shorter of the two wore a dirty blond ponytail. His companion's hair was dark and cropped close to his head. Their deep voices carried from the back of the café. They seemed to know the waitress. She smiled coyly as they placed their orders. The shorter man leaned over the counter and appeared to whisper something to the girl. She laughed nervously as she poured the coffee. It was interesting to watch. *Thank God, those days are behind me*, she thought. It was fun in the beginning. Though good times never last. She took out her purse and left a few dollars by her plate for a tip. Heading for the door, she noticed the taller of the two men turn and stare. She caught his blue eyes. The scent of Old Spice and dried sweat lingered in the air. He gave her a quick wink and lopsided smile. The effect was unexpected. She felt the blood rise to her cheeks. She feigned a smile and quickly made her way to the door.

The wind was fierce. Silence hovered over the town. Small black birds moved through the darkening sky. Heavy humidity suggested a storm. She quickly headed over to her car. The old truck was still blocking her way as she squeezed inside the jeep and started the engine. Rain began to spatter her windshield in a hollow, rhythmic beat. The weather report had not mentioned a storm. It caught her off guard. There were few things she loved more than the changing of the seasons. But, this was not the right time. She could see the boxes and furniture being drenched. It was time to move. If all went well, she could be home within the hour.

Katie headed for the nearest freeway entrance. She drove north heading towards the Napa Valley mountain pass. A few more miles of windy roads would bring her to where she was going. She eagerly started her descent. Her jeep hugged the road with ease. The street began to narrow after about a mile. Cars passed in a blurred, distorted rhythm, and her windshield wipers set pace with the increasing volume of rain. The approaching headlights seemed out of focus in the dim haze. This would not be a passing drizzle. The wind seemed determined. She could feel her jeep struggling against the force of the gusts.

Taking a tight curve, Katie's eyes were drawn to a white, wooden crucifix propped up on the side of the mountain. A bouquet of pink roses had been carefully placed at its base. They were fresh, possibly hours old. The raindrops glistened on the colorful petals like precious diamonds. Next to the roses was a large, cinnamon colored teddy bear. The stuffed animal had fallen on its side and was flecked with mud. Its face appeared to be gazing up to the sky. One eye was missing. The image chilled her to the core. *Focus on your driving. Think about it later.* The inside of the jeep was growing colder as she made her way up the hill. She reached down and turned on the heater.

Warm air filled the interior. The windows began to fog up and the cars driving by became even more distorted. The darkness was disconcerting and out of place for this time of day. It became more difficult to focus. The windshield reflected the distorted lights from the passing vehicles impeding the visibility. She felt disoriented and conceptually disjointed. The first stages of panic descended like soft butterfly wings upon her chest. It was becoming difficult to breathe.

Don't lose it now! It's just a storm! The voice inside her head was frantic. *Focus on your new life. Focus on your new house. Don't think about the jeep losing control and careening off the side of the mountain. You've come so far. Cool it!* She took a deep breath and tried to regain her composure. It took effort not to give into the panic, which was painful and primitive and somehow provocative. She hated to lose control. *Breathe. All right that's better,* she thought. The storm continued. She searched for the final turnoff that would bring her to the last stretch of her journey. Only a few miles of windy roads remained. The redwoods were thick along the edges of the road. After several minutes, she discovered the turnoff and made her way down a narrow dirt road. She followed it as it curved through a dense forest. The jeep's tires struggled against the thick mud.

As the vehicle made its way down the path, the light became increasingly dense and filtered. The trees created a protected canopy. After driving several hundred yards, a clearing emerged. Her little cabin was nestled comfortably among the seemingly endless woods. She guided her jeep toward the front driveway. Her heart raced. This was it. She wanted to make the moment last. Carefully letting herself out the jeep, Katie shut her door, and the sound echoed through the woods. Her white Keds slipped down into the thick mud. She could feel the cold, wet soil filling the spaces in her shoes. The rain continued pouring down. It felt sensual. She breathed in the fresh pine. The fragrance was inviting. The sharp cry of a Stellar Jay rang out from the top of an old oak. "Yes, little one. I hear you," she whispered. An orchestra of sound was emanating throughout the forest. Birds and insects were setting pace. Oh God, this was all so familiar. The simplicity was delightful. The one-bedroom cabin nestled within the heart of the woods.

She walked toward the modest building. Rain rolled down her face like sparkling tears. The dark, wooden logs appeared black from the steady downpour. The cabin was approached with reverence. She climbed up the old, wooden steps. A collection of moss and mushrooms had made their home on the planks of the front porch. Her fingertips moved gently over the wooden beams. She brought her face against the front wall and breathed in the sharp, earthy scent. A slow, deliberate movement caught her attention. A dark purple salamander made its way along the wooden landing. Tiny, golden spots dotted its back and sides. Beads of precipitation covered its moist, delicate body. Katie squatted down on her haunches to get a better view. The little creature's head cocked slightly as its shiny, black eye gazed up at her. After a moment's pause, the tiny amphibian continued its shuffle along the cabin wall. The discovery filled her heart with joy. How many more treasures awaited?

Katie reached into her pocket and pulled out the house key. She carefully placed it into the old-fashioned ceramic doorknob. The door clicked opened. She gingerly stepped over the threshold and went inside. The room was stale and musty. There was a strange, dense quality to the air. For a moment, it felt as if she were inhaling a thick serum, but the sensation was gone as quickly as it begun. She told herself that quite some time must have passed since anyone had stepped foot inside the cabin. It was bound to feel stuffy and slightly oppressive. A thin beam of light was making its way through the curtains above the sink. She walked over and pulled the cord, opening them further. The afternoon light filled the cabin. She grabbed hold of the latch above the window and clicked it open with a dull scraping sound. No doubt a little WD40 would be a welcoming addition to many of the old doors and windows. Breathing in the crisp, clean mountain air refreshed her. She continued her exploration of the cabin.

The layout of the cabin was simple: the main entry room was half the size of the entire house. It was a combination living-room-kitchen area. The great room was eight hundred square feet, laid out in a perfect square. An impressive fireplace was set against the back wall of the room. There was a collection of river stones that had been carefully arranged around the hearth. They rose to the top of the high ceiling, adding to the rustic charm. A kitchen and dining area was located on the opposite side of the room. This space was modest and simple. A large picture window rested above an old farmer's sink. The rusty chrome basin lacked a garbage disposal. She made a mental note to buy a drain catcher. The cabin relied on a well system located at the back of the property.

A collection of cherry wood cabinets surrounded the sink, the counter space allowing just enough room for preparing meals and washing dishes. It was simple and clean. The space was not conducive to a dishwasher. Katie was not concerned. With it just being herself, a few hand-washed dishes would not present a problem. Frayed, white curtains, designed with delicately embroidered flowers, covered the kitchen window. They hung easily on a thin, golden rod. There was a thick coating of dust covering the fabric. A collection of spider webs surrounded the windowpanes. She smiled to herself. Her mother used to call them *Irish Curtains.* The endearing phrase had always made her laugh as a little girl. Spider webs were fascinating creations. The clever patterns were really quite beautiful. The story of *Charlottes' Web* had always brought her to tears. Insects and spiders had never intimidated Katie in the least. They were just one more interesting addition in nature's collection. She made a point to relocate unwelcome insects outdoors. After all, there was no point in hurting something that was simply trying to live its life.

She walked past the kitchen pantry, down a short hallway leading toward the bedroom. The room was as large as the livingroom space. She walked inside and tried to imagine how she would arrange the new furniture. While shopping in the city, she was delighted to discover a beautiful king-size cherry wood bed. It had a gorgeous canopy and delicately engraved headboard. She had purchased a forest green comforter set with matching sheers. The color scheme had always been her favorite. She had suggested it to her ex- husband several times and was met with open contempt. The past echoed in her mind. *We can't afford it. Maybe if you hadn't wasted your time in college painting pictures, you'd have a real job. Your nursery business doesn't pay for shit.*

The memory of Jake's voice turned her stomach. She tried to rid herself of it by focusing on the cabin. The bedroom set included a large wardrobe and matching drawers. By chance, she had stumbled on a modest family-owned furniture store in the Mission District in San Francisco. It had been years since she'd treated herself. If that meant using a credit card or two, so be it. Still, she had been good for so long. Her marriage had seen to that. In the back of her mind she could hear the rough, sarcastic voice of her ex-husband. *Jesus Christ, Katie! Money doesn't grow on trees! What the hell do you need with a fancy-ass bed anyway? Who do you think you are? Queen freaking Elizabeth?*

She shook her head to make the voice disappear. Jake's memory had a way of breaking in at the most inappropriate times.

Her plans for her bedroom collection made her think of her grandmother. She had been a benevolent woman. Some of Katie's most cherished possessions were items she had lovingly passed down. This would be the perfect room to fill with antiques and collectibles. Her set of porcelain animal figurines would go beautifully atop her new dresser.

She walked over to the large picture window. Its southern exposure filled the space with welcoming light. She took a deep breath. The lake could be seen outside in the distance. Golden light highlighted the water. Sunlight caressed the glass warming the room. She was safe. She slid down to the floor like an eager child. Resting on her back, she allowed things to sink in.

The owners of the cabin had offered it under market value. Katie had not wanted to ask too many questions for fear that they would change their minds. She barely slept the night before escrow. The idea that she actually owned fifteen acres was still so overwhelming. She planned to explore every inch of the property.

Much of the land would be used for her nursery. She had started her business, Cozy Crops, a few years after graduating college. She enjoyed selling organic produce at the Bay Area farmers' markets. Her growing grounds were leased in Berkeley. The commute had been over a half an hour's drive from her old apartment. The business grew over the years, and so did her customer base. The money from the nursery and a small inheritance from her mother had allowed her to purchase the cabin and property.

The realtor had pointed out several open spaces on the land that would be perfect for vegetable gardening. She could imagine all of the beautiful heirloom tomato plants growing. Her commute would be just outside in the meadow behind her cabin.

After indulging her daydreams, Katie opened her eyes. She gazed up at the ceiling and noticed a faint outline etched along the overhead beams. The lines appeared to be deep enough to support a small door. The nature of the construction was difficult to determine. There was a considerable glare from what appeared to be varnish.

The glossy coating was thick and concentrated. The reflective quality suggested that it had been recently applied. Whoever had attempted this project did not seem to take much pride in their work. The brushstrokes had been painted haphazardly. They were unusually jagged and edgy. Was it a door to an attic she wondered? Her realtor could have gained some extra selling points. Then again, she'd been sold the moment she stepped onto the property. Katie suspected the agent had caught on to this. Oh well. She would have to take a closer look when she had more time. A ladder would come in handy for the job. Better add it to the list.

She reluctantly sat up and stretched. Her muscles protested. Moving boxes all morning had taken its toll. She made her way across the bedroom and opened the door leading to the full size bathroom. The dark, hardwood floors covered the entire cabin, including the bathroom. They were newly polished and waxed. Several thick rugs would go beautifully next to the dark wood. The mountain air could get very cold and hardwood floors could be unforgiving. As part of the sale's agreement, a new toilet and shower fixture had been installed. They were simple, unremarkable Sears' models. Underneath the chrome shower fixture was a claw-foot tub. The vintage beauty was a wonderful reminder of the past. Her mouth took up the shape of a grin. She loved this little piece of history. It was easy to imagine herself submerged under a thousand warm bubbles with scented candles lighting the room. New towels and curtains would definitely add some warmth to the bathroom. She had the perfect antique table to set next to the tub. It was mahogany wood and would go nicely with the floors. A new painting would brighten up the space as well. A vineyard scene would be nice. The towels would have to match the canvas. The shopping list continued to grow.

After exploring her new home, she headed back outside to her jeep. The air was fresh and clean. It felt light compared to the air in the cabin. The clouds were beginning to gather. The birds and insects quieted their tenacious harmonies. She went through her car hunting for something to prop open the front door. She spotted a small box of books. The container was packed full of classics by Steinbeck, Faulkner, Jane Austen, Stephen King, and Victor Hugo. The novels appeared to be waiting for her. She propped open the door with the heavy box. Success. She planned on re-visiting her old favorites this winter, bundled up nicely in front of the fireplace.

Containers of clothes and personal items were carried to the bedroom. Once they'd reached a considerable height, she opened the closet door. It was a nice walk-in. She pulled a cord that hung from the high ceiling illuminating the space. She would begin the task of sorting and unpacking the items once the movers arrived. Her goal for the moment was simply to move the belongings from the jeep without blocking the path of the new furniture.

She'd just finished moving a box of dishes when she heard the loud, steady motor of the moving van. The sound of cracking twigs and branches echoed in the forest. The van prominently displayed in large black letters, *The Merry Movers*, as it turned in a wide forward arch and slowly shifted into reverse. The driver carefully backed up toward the cabin door and cut the ignition. The doors opened simultaneously. The movers appeared and were surprisingly young. They were tall, with athletic builds, neatly styled blond hair and rosy cheeks. The boys made their way over and introduced themselves. "Hi. I'm Ted and this is my brother, Paul. Are you Katie O'Brien?" He asked, looking down at his clipboard.

"Yes, I am. Thank you for showing up on time. Some of the furniture is pretty big. It might take a few minutes for me to figure out where it should go. I hope you don't mind."

"No problem." Paul spoke up. Wavy blond curls framed a boyish face. He looked young, earnest. "Take your time. This is our last job of the day and we're in no rush," he smiled.

She suggested they start with the heavier items for the bedroom and work their way to the living room. They were happy to oblige. As they headed back to the van, she made her way over to the jeep and searched for a small box marked *kitchen*. She carried it back to the dining room table. Carefully unpacking it, she found her coffee pot buried at the bottom. Sadly, she realized she'd forgotten to pick up coffee beans. She unwrapped her tea kettle instead, filled it and placed it on the stove. After making the coffee, she offered the cups and apologized for the instant coffee. They accepted their drinks enthusiastically, and it warmed her deeply.

Katie soon learned that the two young men were working their way through school, majoring in political science and business respectively while renting a house with two other roommates. They were more than happy to discuss their college adventures. She was impressed by the way they multitasked. They covered a number of subjects as they moved the heavy furniture. Paul Berry was taking political science and history courses at the University. He was very knowledgeable about current political events. Ted Berry, on the other hand, was fascinated by business matters particularly the stock market. He shared several tips with Katie on investing, which she found quite interesting. She asked the right kind of questions, and encouraged the boys to open up and share. Their enthusiasm and banter was engaging.

There was room for Katie to chime in. She had a broad understanding of history, which seemed to impress Paul. By the end of the day, he was looking at her with quiet admiration. They had made the entire move pleasant and enlightening. This was one part of the move that Katie had been dreading. Instead, she had fully enjoyed the experience. They were true to their word. They had waited patiently for her to consider the placement of the furniture. She had chosen to set up the bed against the opposite wall, across from the large, southern exposed window. The position would allow her to wake up with the view of the lake outside her window. A vanity with matching settee had been set up along the sidewall across from the bathroom. She owned a lovely silver antique mirror and brush set that would go beautifully on the table. The set was one of her favorite gifts from her grandmother. She had received the antique on her fifteenth birthday. She looked forward to unpacking it.

The living room area had come together. Paul and Ted moved the sofa sectional in front of the fireplace. The embroidered upholstery was lavender with golden floral accents. Two Victorian styled cherry wood tables were placed on each side of the sofa. Diamond shaped etchings covered their surface. A golden lamp adorned each table.

On the opposite side of the room hung a framed print of William-Adolph Bouguereau's *Psyche*. The painting portrayed Venus' son, Cupid, flying into the heavens with his beloved. The young woman's face glowed ecstatically as she leaned backwards into her lover's embrace. Psyche's lavender gown matched perfectly with the couch. The room possessed an elegant simplicity. The two boys smiled at one another. They obviously took pride in their work. The furniture had transformed the space into a beautiful old fashioned home.

Katie found her purse and wallet. She insisted they take considerable tips for their hard work. They tried to refuse the generosity, but she insisted. Paul gave Katie his business card as they said their goodbyes. His face suddenly became quite serious as he remarked, "Let us know if you need any more help. The homes out here are older than they look." This offer was made in a protective manner.

"Thank you. Actually, I need help moving my greenhouse. Do you have any time at the end of the month?" she asked.

"Sure," Ted answered." We have the last Friday of the month off if that works for you."

"Sounds perfect."

Paul opened his schedule book and took down the appointment.

"Great. You can call me later in the week with the details," He smiled down at her.

The boys waved goodbye. Katie waved back as they headed down the mountain road. She stood in front of her cabin as storm clouds eclipsed the sun.

CHAPTER 3

A golden blanket of light could be glimpsed in the open space above the forest. An assortment of dark thunderclouds gathered in the sky. The cloud formations brought to mind an angry mob from an old horror movie. A few narrow sunlit beams were managing to make their way through the heavily wooded yard. The contrast between the bright rays and dark clouds was divine. The gradual absence of daylight changed the forest into a different world. Birds were engaging in their final harmonies of the day, their calls fading out one by one as they settled into their evening routines.

A high-pitched whine rushed past her ear. Katie quickly swatted the side of her neck. An annoying mosquito was busy helping itself to a free meal. A small, itchy bump began to rise on the back of her skin. Little insects were swarming in transient clouds. They were obviously offspring from the lake behind the cabin.

The aroma of chimney smoke drifted across the woods. It was most likely coming from one of the houses up the road. Her closest neighbors were about a mile away. It was becoming too dark to visit the lake. Better wait until morning. She headed back inside her cabin. The click of the ceramic doorknob locked her in for the night. Darkness slowly worked its way inside. She made her way to the living room, silence embracing her like a lost lover. All of the years of city living had accustomed Katie to a constant exposure of human noises, horns and cars, and shopping carts. She anticipated the sounds that were no longer part of her world. The peace and quiet was soothing. She walked down the hallway and headed into her bedroom.

The antique lamps on the end tables against the bed were made of crème ceramic and decorated with pink flowers. They were turned on next. The soft light complimented the Victorian charm of the bedroom. Paul and Ted had volunteered to help install the matching forest green draperies over her windows in the bedroom. The effect was elegant. A clip from *Gone with the Wind* suddenly came to mind. She pictured Scarlet O'Hara removing the green velvet curtains from her living room in Tara. She used the material to create a fabulous antebellum costume. The thought brought a smile to her face. "Yes, Ms. Scarlet. Fiddly Dee!" she announced to the empty room. The only response was the deep moan of the wind outside her window. Another storm was gathering outside.

Katie looked around the room. Her antiques and new furniture blended together perfectly. The final job for the evening would be setting up the comforter for the new bed. She walked over to the large bedroom window. The darkness outside added to the mysterious aura of the forest. Strong gusts of wind shook the branches and leaves of the old oaks surrounding the home. Venus was just making an appearance in the night sky. The heavenly body seemed to summon her brothers and sisters. The harvest moon appeared impressively large, its moonbeams glowing eerily through the passing clouds. Although the cloud cover impeded the view of the Milky Way, the clarity was still amazing compared to San Francisco, where the stars often appeared muted by the city's bright lights.

She pulled the drapes together and was comforted by the complete privacy of her bedroom. The comforter set had been placed at the end of the bed. She opened the large container and sorted through the contents. The bed coverings felt soft and alluring in her hands. She went to work making the bed. There were several layers to protect her against the cold. The comforter was the crowning glory. Delicately embroidered violets and cream daisies accented a sea of forest green. They matched perfectly with the lamps in the room. Next, she pulled out the delicate sheers. They would be attached to the top of the canopy. This would be a challenge without a ladder. But she was eager to experience the bed in all of its Victorian glory.

She moved the lamp from the right end table and pushed it against the side of the bed. She hastily pulled off her tennis shoes and muddy socks. She climbed atop the end table and hooked the corner of the sheer through the canopy rod. She continued this process until she had worked herself around the other side. There was one more side to finish at the foot of the bed. A large hope chest rested underneath. A wedding gift from her mother. The vintage treasure contained several handmade quilts and linens. Many of the pieces had been sewn and passed down from generation to generation. Katie gently climbed over the chest and was able to reach the last canopy rod. As she pulled the remaining fabric through the hanger of the foot of the bed, her eyes were drawn up to the center of the ceiling. She noticed the strange varnish that had captured her attention earlier in the day. The bed's canopy was lined up right underneath it. Fumes drifted from the ceiling. The deep lines etched in the wooden beams were thick with gloss, and the remnants of a door appeared to have been painted over. Katie wished she had asked the Berry Brothers' opinion about it. She wondered how much space was available above the bedroom. However, she was not sure how to go about removing the varnish. She had spent a considerable amount of money on the move already. This particular job would have to wait.

Just as she was preparing to step down, her head began to swim. For a moment the room spun completely out of focus. She quickly grabbed the side of the top canopy, almost toppling headfirst onto the hardwood floor, steadying herself just in time and lowered herself down from chest to the edge of the bed.

Her body shook and a light film of sweat covered her face and neck. Perhaps it was time to call it a night. What she needed now was a nice hot shower, her flannel pajamas, and a good book. She walked back to the livingroom and turned off the lights. Back in her bedroom, she hunted around for her supplies. Finally discovering her toiletries inside one of the open boxes, she was ready. She made her way into the bathroom and locked the door. The room was exceptionally chilly. She organized all of her creams and facial washes. A set of teal green towels was hung on the rack next to the shower. Her dirty clothes were stripped off and dropped unceremoniously to the ground. She turned on the faucet and the hot water sprayed out in strong, heavy streams. The water pressure was amazing as she carefully stepped over into the claw-foot tub. It had a pleasant, natural odor. Jets of warm water ran down her back and legs, easing the muscles and loosening her tired joints. She poured a generous amount of shampoo in her hair and lathered. She followed it with a lavender scented conditioner. After a considerable amount of time, she reluctantly turned off the shower and dried herself. The new towels felt wonderful on her skin. Afterwards, she applied moisturizers and brushed her teeth. Her flannel pajamas and slippers were like a nice hug. She unlocked the bathroom door and went back into the bedroom. The temperature outside had dropped considerably. Her slipper feet padded down the hallway as she headed over to the thermostat.

The furnace clicked into action. Warm air began to drift inside the room. She discovered her silver brush hidden in one of the boxes next to the closet. She carried it back to the vanity and sat down. She began to run the soft bristles through her hair. The auburn curls flowed down her shoulders with each stroke. There were gray strands mixed in. It had been a long time since she had been to a salon. Perhaps she would treat herself. A little cut and color would be a nice little lift. After all, the house was getting a makeover. Why not get one too?

Katie looked at her reflection in the mirror. Her skin was glowing from the recent shower and pampering. A rosy blush shone on her high cheekbones. A hint of the young girl she had once been gazing back at her. There was something in her eyes that she hadn't seen for a very long time. The look of resignation had been replaced by the beginnings of hope. She stood up and stretched. The box of classic novels was stacked in the corner of the room. She briefly considered her options. Victor Hugo was the obvious choice. *Les Misérables* was a masterpiece. Who could compete with a hero like Jean Val Jean?

She kicked off her slippers and slid under the soft covers. Her petite body had ample room in the king-sized bed. After plumping up her pillows, she dove into her beloved novel. Fifteen minutes later, her eyes were struggling to stay open. After reading a sentence for the third time, she reached over and turned off the light. The moonlight shone through the edges of the curtains. The wind outside whipped against the cabin wall. Rain pattered the windows and roof. A deep-throated frog gently croaked outside the bedroom window. Another answered the call from a distance. Within minutes, a frog choir had taken over the entire yard. She drifted off with the gentle sounds of amphibian love.

CHAPTER 4

Katie was standing in an open field. There were tulips as far as she could see. Their scarlet color was so rich and vibrant that they appeared to be bleeding from their petals. They rested on slender green stems the color of emeralds. She wore a dress of silk white satin. It was old fashioned, elegant. Her long sleeves rolled down her arms and flared out across her small hands. A thin, gold cord was tied gently around her delicate waist. The dress billowed down to the ground in a long, flowing train. Her bare feet softly explored the rich soil and grass. It felt like soft, downy feathers. She reached up and caressed the locket, which hung between her breasts. The gold was cold to the touch. Her heart drummed in anticipation. She had to hurry. It would soon be dusk. Someone was waiting in earnest for her arrival.

She looked into the distance. A circle of cherry trees could be seen on top of the hill. Her bare feet traveled over the soft valley. The tulips rolled gently against the front of her legs and back of her calves. They brushed her skin as she made her way through the meadow. The light was thinning. As she walked across the terrain she became aware that something was very wrong. Looking over her shoulder revealed a vision. What she witnessed made no sense. The tulips behind her were turning into paper. The entire field resembled an aged black and white photograph. The brilliant scarlet flowers had been replaced by black and white. Their solidity began slowly breaking down until they were no more. The wind cruelly whipped through the meadow. The transparent skeletal remains disintegrated until there was nothing left but a vast, deadly void. Her horror mounting, she realized that whatever had transformed the flowers was quickly flowing towards her.

Feeling as though her heart were going to burst, she began to run toward the circle of trees. The tulips snapped under her feet. The ground began to lose its soft, malleable quality. Jagged rocks cut her feet as sharp branches tore at the sides of her legs. Her panic was primitive, raw. The clearing was almost in reach. Her foot caught under a heavy root in the ground. She fell forward with an agonizing force. Her brow struck the hard, solid earth. Blood streamed down the side of her face. Just as she began to lose consciousness, she felt the touch of hands under her back and legs. She was lifted into the air as if she were weightless. As the last of her awareness left her, she heard the voice of a man gently whispering her name in her ear, "Katie, Katie."

CHAPTER 5

The morning sunlight was streaming through the open spaces of her bedroom curtains. Birds were greeting the day with harmonies. Katie opened her eyes, completely disoriented. It took her a moment to realize where she was. Her muscles were stiff from the move. The remnants from last night's dream swam in her head. The images were at once lovely and horrifying. Yet one part remained vivid in her mind, the voice of the man in her dreams was oddly familiar. She could feel the hands even now gently touching her skin. The voice had been so gentle. For a moment, she considered trying to go back to sleep to revisit the dream. No, there was too much to do today. Reluctantly, she got out of bed and stretched. The open curtains revealed a glorious morning. The sun's rays embraced the lake in the distance. This was what she'd been waiting for.

She slipped on her fuzzy bedroom slippers and headed down the hallway. She opened the curtains over the kitchen and dining room windows. Warm sunlight streamed into the cabin. She brought out a coffee mug and prepared the water. A box of Entenmann's doughnuts was in the cabinet next to the sink. There were two chocolate and half of a glazed. She chose the chocolate and placed it on a small serving plate. She took a seat in the nook and enjoyed her breakfast. As the caffeine began working its magic, Katie admired the forest outside the window next to the table.

A large raven rested in the branch of an oak tree. He cocked his head sideways and appeared to be watching something moving down on the ground below. The bird's feathers appeared to have been dipped in black ink. The raven quickly dove down onto the forest floor. It grabbed something under the scattered leaves and flew back to the tree. It quickly gobbled up its prize. Katie wondered what it had caught, perhaps a lizard or other small creature. The raven began to call out with a series of caws. He was obviously proud of his hunting skills. She went back to her kitchen and placed her plate in the sink and quickly refreshed her coffee mug before heading back to her bedroom. She pulled on a pair of jeans and a hooded sweatshirt. Her small feet slipped inside a pair of worn out hiking boots. After hunting for her house keys, she let herself out of the cabin.

It was surprisingly warm considering the recent storm. The sharp scent of pine and forest flora was fresh from last night's rain. She walked past the breakfast nook. The proud raven continued to roost in the oak tree. He did not seem concerned by Katie's sudden appearance. His black eyes followed her as she made her way down to the lake. The forest floor became soggy and muddy as she approached the bank. There was a considerable collection of colorful cattails surrounding the golden water. Several noisy black birds darted between the thick reeds. They called out their love calls. Glimpses of scarlet hues accented their ebony shoulders. They flashed their colorful feathers in hopes of attracting the females. Katie slipped through an opening in the tall willows to get a better view. She noticed several flat sandy areas surrounding the lakebed. The dark water gently lapped up against the sides of the bank. Golden rays highlighted the quiet currents. The water edge was thick with green algae. A large tadpole quickly rose to the surface of the water and took a breath of fresh air. His little mouth formed an inquisitive circle. He seemed to be asking a question. By the size of him, Katie guessed he was a bullfrog tadpole. She imagined that the adorable pollywog was the offspring from last night's amphibian choir. The limbless creature quickly made its way back down to the hazy bottom. A swirling cloud of mud and sediment rose to the surface.

She continued her walk along the bottom of the lake. After trudging through several yards of tangled weeds and pussy willows, a nice flattened bank opened to reveal waterfowl. Canadian geese, mallard ducks, and delicate coots were enjoying the morning sun in their comfortably private area. The large flock balanced as their feathers dried. She tried to move closer to get a better look. The observant waterfowl sensed her soft footsteps. Several mallard ducks and coots rushed noisily back into the water. The geese stood their ground. One goose cried out in agitation.

"Sorry guys. I'm just passing through."

Respectively giving them space as she walked back toward the other side of the pond. The gander was simply trying to protect his female. It was a sweet thought. Katie had read that geese mate for life. She would make it a point to watch them from a respective distance, especially during the mating season. By springtime, fuzzy goslings would be waddling all over the property. After a quick look back, she continued her casual stroll.

One goose stood apart from the group. Unlike the Canadian geese, he appeared quite domestic, perhaps an escapee from a local farm or nearby home. His white plumage was striking in the morning sun. Katie stopped for a moment and studied the bird. He was large with bright blue eyes and a dark, pumpkin-colored beak. From the size, she assumed it was a gander. A collection of gray spots covered his long neck and wings. He gazed back with unusual alertness and intenseness.   After walking several yards, she had the feeling that she was being followed. Looking back over her shoulder, it soon became apparent that the goose was keeping pace from a safe distance.

"Hello sweet thing. Are you following me?"

The beauty of the land was easing her tired mind. She tore herself away from the water's edge. It was time to begin the day's errands.

"Goodbye, pretty goose. I'll see you tomorrow morning."

The gander appeared to understand. She slowly made her way back to the cabin.

After a quick shower and change, she was ready to head into town. After a moment's consideration, she headed back to her bedroom and powered up the laptop. The connection was working just fine. She finished writing down the names of the stores and their quickest routes. Now that she had a point of reference, the day's work seemed less daunting.

The drive back down the mountain was peaceful without a storm to contend with, and the beautiful countryside had been washed clean from last night's downpour. The white crucifix appeared at the bend of the mountain. Bright beams of sunlight solemnly washed over the marker. The teddy bear remained on its side covered in mud.

The town of Napa was bustling on a cheerful Sunday morning. Locals and tourists were taking advantage of the pleasant weather. The downtown area was full of shops and restaurants. The hardware store was first on the list. It was located between a modest hair salon and a used bookstore. The appliance store seemed ordinary, though the inside was a pleasant surprise. Antique Coca Cola signs decorated the walls, and there were several large black and white photographs depicting Napa Valley in the forties and fifties. Freshly picked fruit were available in the entryway. They were divided up between wooden bins, which were built into a large antique table. A silver scale rested on the top shelf. Paper and plastic bags hung on a wooden handle. Old fashioned breadboxes, cutting boards, and kitchen appliances were organized along the shelves throughout the store. Rows of vegetable seed packets lined the walls. Whimsical farm animal figurines and teapots adorned several table displays. The prices had been hand written on small white tags tied with string.

She searched for several minutes looking for her items. A teenage boy with acne shyly directed her over to the kitchen supplies. The back of the store contained the usual collection of hardware tools such as nails, hammers, and painting supplies. She picked out a drain catcher and a large bottle of WD40. She noticed a sales table near the back door. Several Keurig coffee machines were on sale. They were fairly reasonable. Perhaps the store had purchased them in anticipation for the holiday season. *They really have a little of everything*, she thought. The idea of having fresh brewed coffee at the push of a button was just a little too tempting. She quickly lifted one of the boxes closest to her and placed it in her basket. She eyed the coffee and chose the darkest brew she could find.

An elderly woman was helping customers at the front counter. Her silver hair was pulled in a neatly styled bun at the back of her head. The line was taking longer than she expected. As she made her way forward, one more table caught her attention. It was filled with ceramic teapots, cups, and saucers. She reached down and picked up an ivory cup decorated with violets.

As she held it, she recalled a similar looking cup flying past her face, shattering into tiny pieces as it hit the dining room wall. Her eyes burning with tears as she stared at the ruined antique. Her grandmother had passed down the heirloom shortly before she'd died. She'd knelt down in grief, Jake's shadow descending.

Katie's hands shook as she placed the teacup back on its saucer. She took a deep breath and tried to collect herself as the line moved forward. Finally, she had made it to the front register. An assortment of glass jars filled with candies rested on the counter. Old-fashioned saltwater taffies, gumdrops, chocolates, and swizzle sticks filled the containers. She had not seen some of the varieties since she was a little girl. *Might have to add those to the list as well*, she thought. The old woman smiled warmly at Katie. The teenage boy with acne bagged her purchases. He helped her add a pound of mixed candy to the order. The cash register was an old antique, possibly dating back to the twenties. The cashier smiled as the teenage boy continued bagging up the groceries.

"Are you visiting Napa today?" the elderly woman inquired.

"Actually, I just moved here yesterday." Katie answered.

"Oh that's wonderful. I'm Edith and this is my grandson, Carl. It's his first day of work," she added proudly. "My family and I all pretty much grew up in this store."

The owner's eyes were filled with nostalgia as she busied herself ringing up the purchases.

"Be sure to come back and visit us next weekend. We're having a sale on all of our fine china and tea sets!"

"One tea set did catch my eye. It's ivory, with violets."

"Oh yes. That set's from the Galway Collection imported from Ireland."

Katie smiled at the elderly matron. She paid for her things and pushed her cart outside. Carl helped her carry out the new ladder. After her bags were loaded in the jeep, she walked over to the hair salon and peaked through the window. There was a large sign that read, "The Main Event."

Men and women were being treated to haircuts, beauty treatments, and manicures. Everyone seemed to be enjoying their pampering. Several customers were waiting for their appointments. Katie inquired about the rates of a cut and color at the front desk. The prices were quite reasonable. They were booked up for a few weeks. After checking the calendar, the front desk assistant penciled her in and gave her an appointment card.

Next, she headed to a large grocery store a few blocks south of Main Street. Cool air greeted her as the automatic doors slid open. Her shopping had worked up her appetite.

The produce department was in the back of the store. She found the organic section and chose some fresh tomatoes, romaine lettuce, cucumbers, and a large avocado for her salad. Grocery store vegetables did not compare to her homegrown produce, but it would be a few more months before her garden would be ready. In the mean time, she would have to make due. A large salad with some garbanzo beans would be perfect for tonight's dinner. She had some canned beans back at the house. A glass of wine would go nicely with the simple meal.

Katie found the wine aisle and took her time examining the various options. She couldn't decide on red or white. Finally, a rich cab along with a bottle of Napa Valley Chardonnay made the cut. There was a fresh-baked bread display by the cash registers. Perfect. Her grocery cart was soon filled to the top with food and cleaning supplies. It was a nice feeling to stock up on groceries. She was one step, closer to bringing her life to a state of normalcy. She paid for her items and made her way back to her jeep. It was a pleasant ride back to the cabin.

CHAPTER 6

Soft afternoon light spilled through the open spaces of the forest as she turned into her front yard. The leaves of the trees were beginning to turn a mixture of bright orange and canary yellow. The intense colors made her yearn for paints and a canvas. Pulling up to the driveway, she was startled to discover a white van parked in front of her cabin. She was not expecting visitors. Katie parked her car. A gorgeous woman with three children climbed down from her porch steps and smiled happily as they made their way over to the jeep.

The woman appeared to be in her early to mid thirties. She carried herself like a model as she approached. Her face was flawless, youthful. Long black lashes framing her large brown eyes. The color reminded Katie of cups of coffee and love letters. Curly black hair trailing down slender shoulders. A simple red cotton dress flowed to her knees, complimenting her long legs. The color was a contrast to her dark hair and golden skin. The woman was easily six or seven inches taller than Katie. She seemed unaware of her beauty, which made her even more breathtaking.

Two girls and a young boy trailed behind the woman. The older girl appeared to be around thirteen or fourteen. Her features were delicate. Her hazel eyes were bright with excitement. She held a large Tupperware container in her slender arms. Katie remembered how life could be one prolonged adventure at that age. There was a special kind of magic that seemed to light everything.

The younger girl standing next to her sister appeared to be about ten or eleven. Her eyes were dark and almond shaped, very similar to the woman's. She was tall, slender. A small boy of about five or six clenched his mother's hand and peered out from behind her back. Dark, curly locks framed a cherub face. His brown eyes were full of curiosity. He wore a bright green t-shirt, with a picture of a yellow dump truck on the front. It matched his green shorts and tennis shoes. The boy smiled shyly as he stole quick glances at Katie. The woman introduced herself.

"Hello. My name is Camellia Sanchez. These are my two girls, Lizzie and Jessie, and my son Bennie. We live right up the hill," she pointed toward the road with her perfectly manicured hand.

"It's the first house on your right about a mile up. We heard that you just moved in and wanted to bring you over a little something to eat."

Lizzie proudly offered the container with an enthusiastic smile. Katie was moved by the gesture. She figured that their home must have been the one producing chimney smoke last night.

"That is so sweet and thoughtful. My name is Katie O'Brien. I just moved in yesterday from San Francisco."

"Well you will soon find out that it's a lot different up here. Everybody knows everybody," Camellia explained.

The little boy suddenly spoke up.

"There's a chocolate cake in there," he pointed eagerly to the container in his sister's hands. "We helped momma make it!"

From his intense expression, Katie imagined he would like to help eat it.

"Would you all like to come in for a minute? I could use the company."

Camellia smiled at the invitation flashing her beautiful white teeth.

"Are you sure we won't be in the way? I know what a pain moving can be."

"It would be a nice break from my unpacking. Believe me."

Camellia noticed her groceries in the jeep.

"Here, let us help you with those."

Everyone pitched in and grabbed some bags. Katie led them over to the porch and opened the front door. She escorted them over to the kitchen area so they could put the groceries down. The two women worked together and put away the perishables. Afterwards, Katie led the family around her cabin for a quick tour. Camellia offered genuine praise of the home. She was particularly enthusiastic about the forest green color scheme in the bedroom. The family was quite impressed by the collection of beautiful antiques, especially with the delicate porcelain animal figurines. Camellia firmly warned the children not to handle them.

"Oh, that's alright," Katie replied. "I'm sure they know to be careful."

The children took turns gently picking up the antiques. Camellia smiled at Katie's easy way with the children. Lizzie couldn't seem to pull herself away from the beautiful vanity.

"Make yourself comfortable, sweetie. Have a seat," Katie encouraged.

The young girl smiled shyly as she sat down and looked at her reflection in the mirror. She carefully handled the silver brush set. After the tour, Katie led them back to the kitchen and served the chocolate cake with glasses of cold almond milk. Benny giggled throughout the meal and managed to get the majority of his cake on his face, rather than in his mouth. His sisters took turns at wiping him clean.

After dessert, Katie asked the children if they'd like to play in the yard.

"Stay close by and keep an eye on your little brother," Camellia firmly instructed.

"Yes, mommy," the girls chimed in unison.

Lizzie took hold of Bennie's hand and led him out of the house. The women took the plates back to the sink. Katie suggested they could keep a better eye on the children from her large bedroom window. The ladies made small talk for several minutes. Camellia's eyes wandered around the room, taking in the thick varnish on the bedroom ceiling. A puzzled expression came over her face. "That is quite a paint job," she humorously remarked.

"I know, it's strange. I didn't notice it until yesterday. I'm wondering if there might be an attic door underneath all of that gloss."

"Maybe. It's hard to tell. My husband, Steven, is a contractor. He's really handy. If you want, I could bring him by later in the week and have him take a look at it."

Katie was touched at the offer.

"That would be great! I'm curious to know what's up there."

Camellia was quiet for a moment.

"So is it just you all alone up here?"

"Yes," Katie smiled. "It's just me. My husband and I divorced about a year ago. I'm pretty much… starting over."

"No children?" Camellia inquired.

"No. I love them, but it never seemed like the right time to have them."

Camellia nodded understandingly. "I admire you. It takes a lot of guts to start over by your self. Good for you."

"Well, it took a lot out of me to change," she sighed. "But I'm glad I did it."

"I guess I better get everyone back home and help the kids get ready for school tomorrow. I'd love to meet up for some coffee later in the week. There are some nice cafés downtown," Camellia remarked.

"That sounds great! I would love to."

The two women quickly exchanged phone numbers. They headed over to the door to look for the children and were greeted with enthusiastic shouts.

"Mommy! Mommy! Come see the funny goose," the children shouted.

Camellia and Katie opened the door and saw all three children standing next to an old oak. Beside the towering tree stood a large, white goose. He seemed to be sizing up the children.

"Careful. Geese can be mean. Give him some space," Camellia warned.

Katie explained how the goose had been following her around the lake earlier in the morning.

"Thanksgiving is just around the corner. Looks like you already have your main course," Camellia laughed.

The smile quickly faded from Katie's face. Camellia worried that she had offended her new neighbor.

"I'm sorry. I was joking."

Katie could feel the blood rising to her cheeks. "Oh, that's alright," she hastily replied.

She was always very quick to defend animal rights.

"Well, it seems that you're not alone after all."

"Looks that way," Katie smiled.

"Alright kiddos, we better get you back to the house to start your homework."

The girls sighed at their mother's remark. After they'd driven off, she spent the rest of the night unpacking, turning in early in order to start over again in the morning.

CHAPTER 7

The following weeks consisted of unpacking, shopping, and decorating. Each day presented new challenges, exciting discoveries, and a sense of growing peace. Katie began meeting up with her new neighbor every morning for coffee. She looked forward to their daily visits. Camellia introduced her to the best cafés in town. The women quickly bonded and soon felt as if they had been friends for years. At the end of the month, she invited Katie to visit her house for brunch. Katie eagerly accepted the offer.

She was in good spirits as she drove to the house on the top of the hill. She double-checked the address, which she had typed into her phone. It took just a few moments to find the two-story Mediterranean. Grand arches, parapets, and high windows were set off dramatically under a red tile roof.

She parked her old jeep in the driveway and walked down a cobble stone path, which wound through a thick forest of oak trees. The front yard was professionally landscaped, with a collection of colorful, native perennials that included rosemary and lavender. Honeybees hovered over the fragrant flowers. She walked up the front steps and rang the doorbell. The sound of hurried footsteps echoed down the hallway. Katie could see Camellia approaching through a stained glass window. She opened the door and greeted her with a warm embrace.

"Come on in!"

Camellia welcomed her inside and began the grand tour of her well-kept home. The house was considerably quiet with the girls in school and Bennie on a play-date. She proudly explained how her husband, Steven, had built the home from the ground up. He'd orchestrated every detail concerning the electrical, heating, and planning. Katie admired the floor to ceiling arched windows. Each room had a view of the mountains and woods. Their feet echoed across the polished marble floors. They headed into a large livingroom with an enormous eighty-inch flat screen TV, in front of a comfortable sectional and recliner set. A game room was connected. An air hockey table was set up in the corner of the room. Several shelves for toys and puzzles hung on the walls. They were arranged according to subject. It was amazing to see such organization with three children under foot. Perhaps that was why everything seemed to have a place.

Katie noticed several technical gadgets throughout the house.

"My husband is obsessed with technology. Steven is always at the front of the line whenever something new comes out," Camellia laughed.

They headed up the stairs to view the rest of the house. The master bedroom had an arched picture window connected by a Juliet balcony. It looked out over an incredible view of the Napa Valley Mountains. The room was decorated with neutral colors and clean lines. A large painting of a peaceful seascape hung over the bed. A sense of tranquility lingered in the air. Katie noticed several family photographs, which lined the hallway walls. Beautiful, smiling faces displayed lovingly in a collection of vacation and holiday scenes. Bennie's room was packed with toy trucks and cars. A large green and yellow comforter covered his twin bed.

In contrast, the girls' rooms were adorned with pinks and purples. Horse posters, ribbons, and various musical groups covered the walls. The oldest daughter, Lizzie, had replaced some of her equestrian prints with the latest teenage heartthrobs. A One Direction poster hung over her bed. It was easy to see that the she was in that bittersweet boy crazy phase. Katie imagined her mother would have her hands full in a year or two, judging by the girl's pretty features and blossoming curves.

Lastly, they made their way into the guest bedroom. Another great view of the mountains was shown off in the large window across from the queen size bed. A painting of a romantic vineyard hung above the oak headboard. A matching dresser rested on the opposite wall. A large, golden crucifix hung above it. The room was inviting.

Camellia offered refreshments as they walked back downstairs. Katie eagerly accepted. The morning was warm and fresh as they made their way out to the panoramic deck. Camellia brought out coffee and Danishes and set them on the glass table between two comfortable wicker chairs. The family's elderly golden retriever followed the ladies outside. He appeared to be smiling as he panted through his graying muzzle. Bugsy sat down heavily and with a loud sigh. He thumped his tail lazily and snuggled up to Camellia's feet. In a few moments, he was snoring deep in his peaceful doggie dreams.

A lavender breeze drifted through the morning air. The shrill sounds of cicadas buzzing from an enormous oak tree. An old-fashioned tire swing blew lazily under its knotty branches. The two women made small talk as they sipped their coffee and enjoyed the pastries. The conversation eventually turned to marriage and family.

"When did you meet your husband?" Katie asked casually.

Camellia stopped eating and slowly turned away. She studied the woods intently. A look of serious contemplation shadowed her face. Her jaw tightened with a rigid anticipation. She seemed to be weighing a very important decision in her mind. After a few moments, Camellia let out a deep sigh and began,"I was in my sophomore year in college when I met a boy named Taylor. My class load was very heavy that semester. Calculus, biology, and chemistry were just a few of my lab classes. Science had always been my favorite subject. I eventually decided to major in environmental engineering."

Katie smiled, and nodded with interest.

"One of the varsity football players was in my chemistry class. His beautiful face and athletic body really made him stand out. But, besides his handsome looks, there was something dangerous and wild lurking behind his bright, hazel eyes. I had heard whispers from my friends that Taylor was riding on a full football scholarship at the university.

One day after class, he hung around my desk while I packed up my books and supplies. He made small talk as we left the class and admitted he found the course very challenging. I sensed that the class was a struggle for the football player. I was more than happy to tutor him. I found the chemistry course to be challenging but very interesting. But, we did not get very much studying done during our first homework session."

She smiled sadly as the story seemed to awaken some long buried memory.

"The first few weeks of dating were wonderful. There were flowers, dinners, movies. He was always the perfect gentleman. And so it came as a complete shock when his personality began changing. One weekend my roommate decided to visit her parents. I had the dorm to myself. Taylor showed up late that Saturday night with a bottle of bourbon and a basket of strawberries. I had never been a big drinker and was hesitant to try it but I eventually did.

"He dipped the strawberries gently into the whiskey and brushed the fruit over my lips. It was an interesting combination of sweet and sour. Once we'd finished the berries, he went into my kitchen and retrieved two glasses. He poured a generous portion of bourbon into each of the cups. We toasted our drinks together and began to watch the movie. He had brought over Pink Floyd's *The Wall*. The film really set the mood for the rest of the evening. The alcohol started to hit me pretty hard soon after.

"Before I knew it, I had zoned out and had fallen into a kind of fog. I had trouble following the story. Everything seemed far away and out of focus. Halfway through the movie, he began to make advances. It began with kissing and gentle caresses. Soon, we were down on my bedroom room floor making out.

"At first, it seemed no different than other times. I had always stopped him before going too far. Being raised Catholic; I was taught to wait until you're married."

Katie nodded understandingly.

"Many people consider this old-fashioned. I just wanted my first time to be on my wedding night. My body wanted him but my heart knew it wasn't right. In the back of my mind, I began to feel that something was very wrong. He was starting to touch me all over was getting really worked up. I took his hands in mine and asked him to slow down. He pushed my hands away angrily. His behavior was becoming very frightening. I begged him to stop, said that I wasn't ready. He ignored me and continued fondling me. Before I knew it, he had me pinned painfully on the floor with my shorts pulled down and was forcing himself on me. I was horrified when I realized what was happening. The physical pain was terrible, but the worst part was the way my heart and spirit shattered in that moment. When he had finished, he left me trembling on the floor with tears rolling down my face. The shame was overwhelming.

"He seemed oblivious to my pain, acting as if nothing had happened, and left to take a shower. Afterwards, he walked over, kissed me on top of the head, and went back to the movie. I remained on the floor in a complete state of shock. The alcohol was still working and it was difficult to think. Guilt flooded my heart and mind. I blamed myself for drinking too much. I should have never allowed myself to be in that position. Later that night, Taylor held me in his arms and filled my head with stories of a beautiful future together.

"Taylor's embrace was gentle, kind. This was the man I had known. In the end, I allowed myself to believe that we would someday be married. What had happened might be forgiven as a terrible mistake. We both had had too much to drink. I'm ashamed to admit that we continued seeing each other after the incident. We never discussed that night. I tried to put it in the back of my mind and pretend it didn't happen. I wanted the memory to just go away. Of course, it lingered in my waking life, and my nightmares.

"Taylor eventually managed to get me to comply with his desires. After we began sleeping together, his attitude changed. He was preoccupied with my appearance. At first it was little things, like my clothes or makeup. "Maybe you should go with a more natural look," he would ask when he saw me touching up my lipstick. "Do you think its appropriate for tonight?" if he thought my dress was too short. He avoided spending any time with my friends and family. When Christmas break rolled around, he seemed strangely preoccupied. He was moody, anxious, and increasingly short tempered.

"It might be a good idea for us to stay in town for winter break," he suggested. "We can spend Christmas together. It will be romantic." I agreed to his request even though my family was heartbroken when they heard the news that I would not be joining them for the holidays. Christmas was always a huge celebration at my house, beginning with Midnight Mass the night before. Before I knew it, Taylor had become involved in every decision I made. My school courses, my major, the clothes I wore-it all seemed to be judged and navigated by him. Nothing I did seemed good enough, I was no longer certain of anything."

Camellia seemed to withdraw inward for a moment and slowly worked her way out.

"This went on. One evening, after a particularly short session of lovemaking, I made a remark about how quick he had been. The comment was intended to make him laugh. Instead, he just stared at me. I'll never forget the look in his eyes. They were no longer human. He slapped me hard across my face. My nose began to bleed all over his satin sheets. I was in complete shock. It was as if it were happening to someone else. He stormed out of the room, and left me sobbing on the bed.

"I had always told myself that I would never allow anyone to lay their hands on me. For days after the incident, I refused to take his calls or return his messages. At the end of the school week, I returned to my dorm room to discover an enormous flower arrangement sitting in front of my door. There was a small card attached. It read:

"Camellia, Please forgive me. I love you more than life itself. I will spend the rest of my days making up for hurting you. Please call me. Love, Taylor."

"I wish that I could say that I never spoke to him again. The flowers should have been tossed in the trash along with his pathetic card. But I loved him. I know how it sounds. It's so hard to say these things aloud. I eventually broke down and called him. He begged me not to leave him. It would never happen again. He told me that he had simply lost control. His football buddies had talked him into taking some steroids. They were all doing it. It had been a huge mistake. There were many promises that it would never happen again. The steroids, he insisted, had been flushed down the toilet. It was convincing argument and it gave me hope. He had only lost control because of drugs. He just wasn't himself.

"Once the steroids were no longer an issue, we could go back to our life together. I desperately wanted to believe him. A few more weeks passed without incident. We had fun and he was back to his old, romantic self. Everything seemed like it would work out. I tried to put the past behind us. As our days began to settle down into a comfortable routine, we made plans for a New Year Eve's party. Some of my classmates had invited us. The night of the party, I noticed he was acting very strange. He was loud and animated trying desperately to be the life of the party. Some of his football buddies showed up later in the evening. At some point, he wandered off with them. It was almost midnight. I waited impatiently for him to return. The countdown to New Years started with my fellow students cheering and singing.

"Everyone was anticipating the ball dropping in Times Square. We were all trying to watch it on the television. One of my good friends, Gary, from my statistics class, put his arm around my shoulders and gave me a quick kiss on the cheek as the clock struck twelve. He soon joined the group of students singing Ald Lang Syne. Their inebriated voices rang out loudly to the music. I tried to make my way out of the room with all of the celebratory students blocking my way. I eventually found my way out and discovered Taylor standing alone in the corner of the kitchen. He was pouring himself a large gin and tonic. He seemed subdued, withdrawn. We eventually left the party together and headed back to his apartment.

"Once inside, I asked him if everything was all right. At first he wouldn't answer me. I insisted, and he became enraged and accused me of flirting with my classmates at the party. Taylor suddenly stood up from his bed and shoved me backwards. I ended up tripping over this duffle bag. My ankle twisted as I landed on the floor in shock and pain."

"I know you've been sleeping around."

"What are you talking about?" I cried.

"You're more trouble than you're worth. I don't know why I ever put up with your bullshit! There are so many prettier and smarter girls that I can be with. You're completely worthless."

"He looked at me with disgust. His words were like daggers. They pierced my heart and soul. My body trembled with shock and confusion as he continued to scream and call me names. I will never forget the terrible things he said to me that night. The attack was much more brutal that the time before. He started slapping and hitting me all over my body. His face was a mask of rage. A piece of me died that night.

"I tried to leave him that night and the night after, but he always found a way to pull me back in. Days turned to weeks and the abuse became regular. At some point, his apologies stopped altogether and I feared for my life. I'd become trapped in a bizarre cycle of love and hate.

"The abuse lasted a couple more months. Then he was gone. A major NFL team had picked him up. Once in a while, I'll catch his name while my husband and his buddies are watching football. Well, anyway, Taylor had no idea that I was a couple of months pregnant, with his child, when he left us. I decided to drop out of the university before the end of the school year. There was a part of me that worried that he would come back to find me. I moved to a neighboring town and met Steven a few months later. He was working on a contractor's assignment in my apartment complex. I was exhausted from working two jobs and barely making ends meet. Steven reminded me of a big teddy bear. It didn't seem to bother him that I was carrying another man's baby. I expected him to wake up one day and realize that he had made a terrible mistake. But he never did. All he wanted to do was love and take care of us. His gentle and caring nature soothed my soul. I finally found peace that I was truly loved and respected.

"I could tell that his parents were not thrilled about me in the beginning. Steven didn't seem to care. They didn't really warm up until I delivered my second child. We were married two weeks before Lizzie was born. A simple courthouse ceremony, my belly was huge, I couldn't even see my shoes. But, I wouldn't change a single moment. Steven's an amazing man, and I thank God every day for sending him to me."

Camellia slowly stopped speaking as her voice began to choke up. The two women's eyes locked. A door quietly opened between them. Katie gently took Camellia's hand and praised her for surviving the abuse. She smiled back with relief. Katie's own fears and regrets about her failed marriage eventually poured out in a flood of words. She couldn't get them out fast enough. There were so many things she'd kept bottled up over the past few years. Camellia's eyes understood when Katie spoke of Jake's verbal and physical abuse. The new friends talked for hours. They bonded over the pains of the past and rejoiced in the hopes of new beginnings. After the two women exhausted themselves in conversation, they quietly smiled at one another. Camellia reached over and gave Katie a fierce hug.

It was close to lunchtime when they headed back to Camellia's kitchen. Their emotional talk had worked them both into a ravenous state of hunger. Enchilada ingredients were quickly organized on a colorful marble counter top. Katie shyly admitted how challenged she was in the kitchen, and the fact that she was a vegetarian. This did not phase Camellia in the least. A variety of cheeses, vegetarian beans, fresh vegetables, and pressed corn tortillas were set together.

Katie was amazed and responded, "Are you prepared for anything or what?"

"I got the impression you were a vegetarian when we first met. I thought you were going to faint when I said that your goose would make a nice Thanksgiving dinner," she laughed. "Don't worry about being inexperienced in the kitchen. You'll be just fine."

Soon the aroma of melting cheese and enchilada sauce filled the room. Camellia reached down under the counter and pulled out a large blender. Margarita mixes and tequila were placed alongside it.

"We're making margaritas too?" Katie asked excitedly.

"It's my hubby's day to pick up the kids from school. Bennie is on a play date with my friend's son. Steven is planning to take them out to ice cream afterwards. The ladies are going to blow off some steam this afternoon!"

They both giggled like teenagers as they salted their glasses and blended their drinks.

CHAPTER 8

Brunch turned into lunch. Staying longer than she had intended, Katie headed back to her cabin in the late afternoon. The excitement from the day's adventure with Camellia had exhausted her more than she'd realized. Her appetite had been happily satisfied by the enchiladas and margaritas. It was a combination that worked magic for her mind and body. She could definitely get used to her friend's home cooking. Some longer workouts would have to be added to her running schedule to keep up with the extra calories. Perhaps she would even get a taste for cooking herself. Stranger things had happened. The thought brought a smile to her face. It was exciting to connect so quickly and intimately with her neighbor. It seemed strange but it was as if they had been friends forever. Feeling calm, she decided to end her day earlier than usual.

Darkness descended on the woods and another day came to an end. The sunset reflected a kaleidoscope of vibrant colors through her bedroom window. She hurried through her nightly routine quicker than usual that evening. The tequila was beginning to make her sleepy. She slipped into a pair of baby blue pajamas; turned up the thermostat in her hallway, and headed over to the kitchen cabinets. A warm cup of almond milk and hot chocolate was ready in a few minutes. Several frogs were beginning their nightly chorus outside the window. The natural harmonies eased her mind and body. She climbed into her warm bed and read a few chapters of *Les Misérables*. Her hot chocolate was rich and creamy. Soon she was falling asleep to the sounds of nature's orchestra.

Sometime later that night, an enormous wave of sound and light exploded in her cabin. Her eyes were met with radiant color prisms emanating from the ceiling above her bed. In a state of panic, she attempted to sit up and was greeted by another burst of light and sound. Her bedroom shook with the momentous force of the blast.

Radiant beams danced in front of her eyes. She finally managed to climb out of bed. She braced her hand on the bedpost. The noise was deafening.

It soon became evident that she wasn't alone. A tall figure stood by the entrance to her bedroom. An engraved pocket watch hung on a small chain attached to his vest pocket. The silver timepiece reflected the soft moonbeams that whispered through her bedroom curtains. She tentatively approached the figure. The mysterious visitor's features became more defined with every step. A bright spectrum of light emanated from his dark silhouette. He eyed her patiently as she moved in closer, gazing at his form. His piercing eyes stirred something in her. They were a dazzling mixture of sapphire blue and emerald. They seemed to belong to the sea. Their stunning color was celestial. She was losing herself in his gaze.

Slowly she found her voice.

"Who are you?" she asked breathlessly.

His mouth turned up slightly at the corners as she questioned him. A radiant and mischievous smile moved over his face. He was handsome, and Katie began to lose her nerve. The shock loosened its hold on her trembling body. As she started to regain her bearings and move backwards, he reached forward, setting his strong hands on her delicate shoulders. His touch brought an intense sensation unlike anything she had experienced before. Powerful arms clasped at the small of her back. At the same time, glossy, black-feathered wings emerged from behind his shoulders, permeating the room. Prisms of light radiated from their tips. What followed was deafening. She feared that her cabin would collapse from the intensity of the blast. The aroma of redwood and honeysuckle filled her bedroom. The intimacy of his embrace left her breathless and wanting more, despite her fear and confusion. Light and sound pulsed so that she was forced to close her eyes. The stranger pulled Katie's small frame tightly against his muscular form.

Even in her shock and confusion, she had time to notice how their bodies complimented one another. Again, their eyes locked. Suddenly the room fragmented, imploded, and was no more.

CHAPTER 9

She found herself sitting in the middle of a vast field of flowers surrounded by dense forests. Cherry trees glowing with the most vivid crimson colors dotted the landscape. The sound of rushing water emanated from the background. A collection of wildflowers and scarlet tulips covered the field. Their rich hues were unusually vibrant. A heavy mist drifted across the outer edges of the meadow. A roaring thunder exploded in the distance. The sound was layered with echoes of hoof beats. From the blanket of dense fog, a vast herd of animals materialized. A large number of zebras made their way across the prairie. Their black and white patterned coats glistened in the foggy background. A stallion was leading the group of mares and foals. Steam rolled from his flared nostrils as he whinnied and charged forward. The procession obediently followed their leader as he increased his stride.

Logic told Katie to get up and run away as the animals approached, but her body refused. The animals closed the distance with frightening speed. The wind whipped and roared with the drumming of hoof beats. The musky aroma of the wild beasts filled the air. Their pace gradually slowed as they approached the row of cherry trees tucked inside the meadow. They finally came to a complete stop with their stallion leading the way. The zebras raised their heads and sniffed at their new surroundings. Their eyes were fixed on Katie. After a moment, the proud stallion stomped the ground with his front hooves and whinnied a loud call that echoed through the valley. Several mares dropped their heads in unison and began to graze the lush, wild grasses. The leader slowly sauntered over to the flowing stream in the meadow. His muscles twitched and moved with each stride he took. A thick layer of sweat clung to his coat. He made his way over to Katie and stood gazing inquisitively over her.

She looked up at the magnificent animal and became lost in the moment. The stallion leaned down until his head was just inches away. Disregarding common sense, Katie reached out her hand to touch his face. It was coarse, hot, and strangely familiar. His blue eyes glowed in the soft, morning light. The handsome animal snorted and steam emanated from his flared nostrils.

The zebra turned his body sharply and retreated into the meadow. His mares and young offspring followed behind him in an orderly procession. The sound slowly faded as the herd vanished into the foggy plains. The experience left her feeling as if the past, present, and future had somehow collided. She was abruptly brought back to reality as the sound of approaching footsteps echoed behind her. Strong hands suddenly rested on her slender shoulders, gently turning her around.

She found herself face to face with her unusual companion. He softly turned her chin upward until their eyes locked. Time dissolved. Their lips brushed against one another. The sensation was like liquid fire, engulfing her in an absolute passion and sublime ecstasy. Gently taking her hands, he guided her to the ground. In a moment, she found herself sitting on his lap. Her small frame was the perfect compliment to his tall and powerful stature. It was so easy to become lost in his unearthly presence. For once, she did not fight her desire. Instead, she relished it and wanted more. He carefully traced his fingers against her throat. His sensual lips followed the curve of her neck. She felt the coarseness of his jaw and inhaled his scent. It was as if the forest, wind, and rain radiated from his pores. She would have given herself entirely to him.

She had been taught from an early age that Catholic girls did not indulge in such reckless, wanton behavior. For a moment, she wondered if angels counted in this moral dilemma. Again, her anxious mind had gotten in the way of a perfect moment. The celestial being studied her with an intensity that made her head swim. Amusement suddenly registered on his face. To her embarrassment, she was almost certain that he had read her thoughts. Color rose to her cheeks. He slowly reached his hand down and brushed one of her auburn curls from her forehead. The impish grin reappeared.

"You need to go back, my dear. You'll need your strength and rest for all I have planned for you."

His thick Irish accent gave her chills. He winked and stepped back. Katie looked up in confusion, wondering what she had almost let happen. He inhaled deeply as his glorious wings stretched, and unfolded. The rich aroma of redwoods filled her senses. Darkness followed and they were gone.

CHAPTER 10

Sunlight fell through the curtains of her bedroom. Waking up gently to the harmonies of the songbirds, she rose slowly from her comfortable bed and made her way to the bathroom. Passing the vanity mirror, she was alarmed at her reflection. Katie stepped back and gazed at the startling rosy cheeks and glowing porcelain skin looking back at her. Worry lines appeared softer and less obvious. Vivid green highlights radiated beautifully in her bright eyes.

What was this? The mountain air could not have been responsible for such a sudden change in appearance. She was afraid to trust her own reflection. It was as if a peace had washed over her. A wave of conflicting emotions weighed on her mind from the night before. She desperately needed to make sense of it. She quickly dressed, grabbing an old worn out pair of sweats and a pink t-shirt. Her hair was tied in a ponytail with a terry cloth band. Strangely, her curls seemed thicker this morning. She only had to wrap the band once. Turning forty had robbed her of so many vanities, including the volume of her once generous locks. She took out her favorite pair of Mizuno running shoes from the bedroom closet.

Katie hurried into the kitchen to grab a cup of coffee. Her new Keurig machine whirled into action creating a perfectly steamy mug. Her instant coffee days were a thing of the past. After a few sips, she grabbed an energy bar and was out the door. She inhaled the crisp mountain air and was invigorated. The breeze brought goose bumps to her arms and chest. That would pass quickly as her run progressed. The cold air moved through her lungs. Painful at first, running was always a mixture of pain and pleasure. It was the perfect metaphor for life.

The morning drowsiness slowly lifted. Every breath heightened her senses and brought her back to herself. She made her way up a moderate hill. It led to an open running path surrounded by beautiful woods and meadows. Katie had happily discovered the worn-out trail earlier in the week. Having your own backyard running area was unheard of in the city. This was just one more perk of country living. As she made her way past the lake, she spotted the old gander by the reeds. He lifted his head and eagerly waddled in her direction. His enthusiasm and excitement brought a smile to her face. It was funny to realize that the one constant male presence in her life was a goose. *Oh well, beggars can't be choosers*, she thought. Then again, was he the only significant man in her life? What exactly had happened last night?

"It was a dream, Katie. Nothing more. Your imagination has gotten the best of you," she spoke aloud to the forest.

Yet, this dream was unlike anything she had experienced before. Her dreaming life was definitely creative at times. Her overactive imagination often surfaced in her sleep. Fragmented images teased her mind. There was a certain sense of urgency that needed to be addressed. The magical meadow had seemed strangely familiar. It was as if something very important had been left behind. With the vibrant recollections of last night's adventures, Katie increased her stride. Calf muscles stretched as her lungs protested the cool, mountain air. The workout was invigorating, and yet painful. In this moment of sheer strain and exertion, she realized that running and romantic love were the same thing. Both were urgent, thrilling, and too often painful and exhausting. Her romantic adventures did not always start off this way. Though they had often gone down in flames or, to a lesser degree, slow burning embers.

Her mind wandered back to the night before. It was just a dream. Wasn't it? But she couldn't help wondering what had actually happened. If it was a dream, and what else could it be, then was she losing her mind? There was a history of mental illness in her family. Come to think of it, there were more members of her family with mental issues than she would like to admit. She remembered in vivid detail her Aunt Mara. The sweet woman had been utterly convinced she was Elizabeth Bennert, the heroine of Jane Austen's novel, *Pride and Prejudice.* Regardless of how the family tried to appease her, she would not sit down to family dinners until they readied a plate for her suitor Mr. Darcy. She often grew angry if the family did not engage her invisible friend in cheerful conversation.

The bizarre flashback sent a chill down her spine. Is one ever conscious of losing their mind? Did it happen slowly or all at once? Katie did not like where this was going. Usually, her thoughts during her runs were carefree. But not today. Her mind once again revisited last evening's dream. It was not just a dream. She'd gazed up into those amazing eyes before. When? How? Why? She couldn't answer. And yet something remarkable had transpired. She was certain of this. There was no rational explanation, but her desire for this man was undeniable. Or was he an angel? What was the deal with his wings? What did he want from her? More importantly, what did she want from him? A few scenarios rushed through her mind bringing a blush to her face. Was this just loneliness from being in a new environment, away form the city? She had not been feeling lonely; she had her new neighbor and family.

As her mind wandered, Katie realized that she had run past her four-mile mark. She could gauge her runs with certain landmarks on the property. An old oak tree reminded her that she would be looping back for the second half of her run. Sweat beads formed on her forehead and underarms. The morning sun was rising as the songbirds were piping up for the harmonies of the day. Her mind and body was flowing with energy. These were the moments that she looked forward to during her workouts. Running often involved pain and exertion, but was rewarded with moments of pure bliss. It was just like life itself.

As her breathing set pace with her strides, she noticed animal tracks on the trail. They were very strange. She could not imagine any animal they would belong to in this part of the country. On the one had, they appeared to be hooves. And yet they were too large and elongated to belong to a deer. The animal would have to be considerably heavy. The prints were set deep within the ground. It was not logical. They were the strangest prints that she had ever seen.

She had done a fair amount of hiking in her life, and was familiar with several kinds of animal tracks in California. She had never come across anything even remotely similar to these prints. The tracks continued along the trail as she turned the corner and made her way back to the house. Something about this was very wrong. It left her with a feeling of dread. She realized that the tracks were continuing the entire second half of her run.

She closed in on miles five and six and the prints followed the course. As she approached the last tenth of a mile, the tracks had trailed off across the yard, and to her dismay, appeared to be leading to the back of the cabin. She slowed her last few strides and arrived at the end of the trail. Sweat beads rolled down her back, thighs, and calves. Her heart raced. She took a deep breath to help even out her breathing. A small voice in her head told her to leave it alone and go back to the front of the house. *Nothing to see here, Katie. There is no reason to try at playing Nancy Drew at this stage in your life,* she thought. The other part of her mind demanded she investigate. Surely the animal had gone back into the woods.

Sparkling drops dripped from the trees and shrubs lining the backyard. Vapors of steam rose into the morning sky. The rich and intoxicating aroma of honeysuckle filled the air. Vines and tendrils trailed throughout the entire back portion of her yard. Some were making their way up the side of the back wall. The result was a natural lattice invading a large portion of the backyard. She noticed that several of the vines and tendrils had been severed. Blossoms and shoots were scattered about. There was something hostile about the way they were laid out on the ground. It would have taken some force to cause this much damage. The vines were so thick in some areas it was difficult to walk behind the cabin.

The tracks continued to make their way closer to the house. Her heart was now pounding so loud in her ears that she felt it might actually explode. Shaking and afraid, she inspected closer and realized that the prints led all the way to the back of her home. This realization was absolutely surreal. Surely she was not seeing this. Something had been left under her bedroom window, a burlap bag, old and torn. *Leave it, Katie, Just walk aw*ay. She stood for a moment in silence. The lonesome, mournful call of a morning dove sounded from the top of her cabin. The cry echoed in the woods. She felt very alone. After gathering her thoughts and taking a deep breath, she decided that ignoring the problem was not the answer. She knew that she had to see what was inside the bag.

Her right hand made the sign of the cross; she uttered the words, "In the name of the Father, the Son, and the Holy Spirit."

With trembling hands, she reached down and picked up the burlap bag. Cautiously, she attempted to open it. It was tied with a loose, gnarled old rope. Finally she was able to free the ropes and open the bag. It took a moment for her eyes to adjust to what was revealed inside. With shaking hands, she reluctantly reached down into the burlap sack and touched the contents inside. Her hands came in contact with a soft, damp object. On closer inspection, she made out what appeared to be a stuffed animal. She slowly pulled the object out and held it by the back of its neck. It was an old stuffed teddy bear. The dirty toy was covered in mold. She turned the bear over in her hands and examined its face. Several areas of the fur had worn off. Stuffing could be seen emerging under the surface. Tattered remnants of fur stuck to her fingers as she handled the toy. A sickening feeling slowly rose through her chest. The mouth of the bear appeared to be pouting. Its right eye was missing. The left eye was black and shiny. It seemed to be staring up in disapproval. The hairs on the back of her arms and head immediately stood on end. The memory was just on the surface of her mind, teasing her, daring her to remember.

"Oh my God," she whispered to herself.

The realization was chilling. She knew with dreadful certainty that this was the same stuffed animal she had seen propped up against the wooden cross, just down the street from her cabin. She had only glimpsed the shrine for a brief moment. And yet the image had burned a vividly disturbing space in her mind. Was this some kind of joke? Perhaps a teenage prank, or was it something more dangerous? Fear and anxiety settled in her chest. Numerous possibilities surfaced in her mind. Each scenario was more troubling than the last. The realization that someone had been lurking outside her bedroom was unimaginable. When? The only evidence was the bear, some strange tracks, and the damage to her honeysuckle vines. Had the bag been dropped when she was asleep, taking a shower, reading her book? The idea left her feeling ill. Her brand new home and sanctuary had been tainted and spoiled. Tears blurred her vision. She had worked too hard, and overcome too many obstacles in her life to be unraveled by this terrible moment. She'd be damned if she were going to let someone ruin it now. Angrily grabbing the burlap bag and bear, she stomped over to the garbage bin at the side of the cabin. Quickly removing the container's lid, the bizarre creature was tossed inside the plastic trashcan. She closed the container and headed back to the front of the house, sprinting up the stairs, unlocking the door, and letting herself inside. The door slammed shut behind her.

With a heavy heart, she rushed to the back of the cabin and made her way into the bathroom. She turned the faucet on high, pumped several squirts of liquid soap from the dispenser, and lathered her hands and arms. The scent of lavender filled the room. The aroma was pleasantly refreshing and clean after handling the putrid stuffed animal. Katie allowed the water to pour over her hands for several minutes until she could no longer take the intensity of the heat. She dried off her hands on a soft white hand towel above the bathroom sink. There was a sense of being on autopilot as she stripped off her sweaty running clothes and dropped them in the hamper. Her body was chilled from a cold sweat that covered her skin in a thin film. She gathered her shower supplies and grabbed a pair of jeans and white satin blouse from her bedroom wardrobe and headed back to the bathroom. The porcelain surface was surprisingly cold on her feet as she stepped inside and pulled close the curtains. Within moments, warm water comforted and soothed her body. The jet spray eased her muscles. After a long, hot shower, and quick clothing change, her hair was blow-dried and brushed out and she was calm.

She rifled through her makeup collection and chose some light, pastel shades to compliment her fair complexion. Her skin was glowing from her morning run. The dark circles under her eyes had faded considerably over the last few days. The foundation could wait for another day. She applied some dusty pink blush to her cheeks and powdered her eyelids with an attractive shade labeled *Mountain Orchid*. She traced around her eyes lightly with a dark brown pencil. Her mascara brushed over her lashes and brought out their volume. Finally, she covered her lips with a dash of plum lipstick. It gave her a fresh, youthful appearance. A light spray of her favorite perfume completed her primping session. Katie grabbed a mauve colored cardigan sweater from her bedroom closet and headed over to the kitchen. The car keys were hanging from the kitchen hook right below a rooster wall clock. A gentle breeze moved over her skin as she made her way outside.

The weather had warmed up quite a bit since her morning run. The air was saturated with the aroma of oak trees and honeysuckle. A beautiful day was in the making. Her mother had once lovingly referred to these kinds of memorable days as *sparkle days*. It was one of her many endearing terms that she used to describe the more important things in life. God, she missed her so. It had been three years since her passing. Time did not ease the loss. The pain was always hovering there at the surface.

She reached for her sunglasses inside her purse and headed to her jeep. Breakfast and plenty of strong coffee was the first order of business. Perhaps it would be a nice idea to try out the new café she had spotted on Main Street the day before. On her way, she made a point to check out the cross and shrine. Three miles into the drive, there was still no sign of it. Strange. It should have appeared by now. It was only mid morning and yet she wanted this day to be over already. Bizarre did not even come close to describing the events that had transpired. After arriving at the Main Street turn off, her jeep followed the road until the café appeared. The sign above the entrance read *The Morning Dew Drop*. A parking space was available directly in front of the door. She quickly maneuvered her jeep into the spot. She headed to the café and let herself in the front door. The walls of the little shop were lined with a variety of paintings from local artists. Many of the artworks depicted vineyards and landscapes. One canvas caught her eye. Canadian Geese flying gracefully over a beautiful Napa Valley winery. It suddenly occurred to her that geese normally flew South during the fall. Her little gander was too heavy to fly with the rest, she realized. Well, he was definitely welcome to stay as long as he wanted. Truth be told, she was beginning to become quite fond of the little guy. Perhaps it was time to give him a name.

Katie took her time admiring the paintings. The rich art and culture of San Francisco was what had originally lured her to the Bay Area. Art galleries and museums seemed to pop up on every corner of the city. After looking at the collection, she approached the front register. Bright orange and white pumpkins decorated the café. The gourds were paired with a variety of old fashion Halloween decorations. Smiling skeletons, witches, and black cats adorned the back wall.

A young man in his early twenties greeted her with a smile. She looked at the chalkboard specials and ordered a cup of lentil soup and side salad. There were several vegetarian options available. She added a soy pumpkin latte with an extra shot of espresso to her order. She would need some caffeine after her morning adventure. She was given a number on a bright green table sign. The server's gaze lingered on her just a little longer than necessary.

She found a nice table by the window. A few minutes later, the enthusiastic waiter brought her soup, salad, and coffee. He looked at her for a moment, flashed an impressive smile, and slowly headed back to the front counter. *That was interesting*, she thought. *Maybe, I'm turning into a cougar*, she mused. She reached into her purse, brought out her compact and lipstick, and did a quick touch up on her lips. She caught a glimpse of her reflection and was surprised by the glowing and youthful appearance. Halfway through her meal, the front door opened with the rush of the warm, morning breeze.

To her surprise, Camellia and Bennie headed into the café. Katie waved at them as mother and son smiled in unison.

"Hello Katie, it's great to see you," Camellia remarked happily.

Bennie smiled shyly and quickly looked down at his brand new light up tennis shoes. Bright neon flashed with each step he took. Katie offered them two seats, which they happily accepted. Camellia ordered herself peppermint mocha and a cup of cocoa for her son. The back of the café had a couple of play tables for children. Bennie was eager to explore all of the books and toys. She set him up with his drink and a couple of picture books and puzzles.

Camellia sat down next to Katie and stripped off her navy pea coat. She sported a pair of sleek navy slacks, shiny red ballerina flats, and a blue and white striped satin blouse. She had accessorized the outfit with small gold loop earrings and a rope necklace. The attractive woman looked like she had just come back from a fashion shoot.

"You look like you should be standing on a yacht drinking champagne in that outfit," she said admiringly.

"I just need to find myself a yacht and a nice bottle of champagne," was Camellia's response.

"Let me know if you do. I'd love to join you."

Their playful banter erupted into a fit of loud giggling. An elderly couple sitting at the front counter turned around to eye them with an irritated indignation. This only made the women laugh harder. Their laughter eventually trailed off as they continued making light conversation.

"I just finished dropping the girls off at school. I figured that mommy deserved a coffee break."

She leaned back in her chair and took a sip from her coffee mug, studying her with a look of approval.

"I have to say…you look very lovely this morning, Katie."

She blushed at the compliment and thanked her. The two women chatted for several minutes until Camellia paused and looked directly in her eyes, "Is everything all right, Katie?"

She was surprised at her intuition.

"Well, if you really want to know, I've had one hell of a morning."

It was a relief to let it all out. A burden was lifted as she quickly told her about the strange encounter. She explained the early morning run, finding the tracks in the field, and the burlap bag and teddy bear left outside her bedroom window, and even mentioned the memorial marker along the side of the road. The details of the angelic visitor were, however, omitted from the story. That subject was a little too personal, as she needed to process the experience. It was something Katie was not ready to share.

Camellia studied her with quiet concern.

"I don't like it. No. I don't like it at all. Yes, it could be harmless teenagers or some prank, but even so, it doesn't sit well with me. It gives me a strange feeling."

Katie's heart was warmed by the concern and protective nature of her new confidant.

"I'm going to mention it to my husband, if you don't mind. Perhaps he can get you fixed up with the latest security system."

She did not mind. In fact, the thought brought a sense of relief. It was embarrassing that she'd not thought of it herself. Being a single woman living alone, she no longer had the luxuries of a secure apartment. The ladies continued chatting until Bennie came running up to their table with a drawing in his hand.

"Katie, I drew you a picture!"

Katie smiled brightly as the child held up his drawing. Her eyes widened in disbelief, as she looked closer. The boy's drawing had two figures in it. The taller image appeared to be a man with blue eyes and dark hair. Next to him stood a short woman with red hair and bright eyes. Both smiled happily together. The only unusual part was what was drawn above the man's shoulders. Two large, black wings flowed out from behind his back. Katie's heart began to race as she held the drawing in her hands.

"That's your angel friend, Katie. He's really nice!"

Katie couldn't find her voice, though she continued to stare at the image. After a moment, she was able to respond to the little boy.

"That's so beautiful, Bennie. Thank you so much for my wonderful drawing," she smiled down at him. He grinned, happily.

"Well, that's my Bennie for you. He has quite the imagination," Camellia laughed softly.

"He sure does," Katie answered quietly.

She was slowly recovering from the shock, and it took effort to sound normal when she spoke.

"I think your son is quite the artist."

"Thank you," Camellia responded. "It's nice that angels are watching over you, Katie. That's a beautiful thought," she smiled. "Well, we better be on our way. I have a few errands to run before lunch."

Mother and son waved their goodbyes and headed out the door. Katie put the drawing in her purse. She was careful not to bend it. It would be placed on her refrigerator when she went home. The image caught her completely off guard after last night's dream. She was not sure what to make of it. Maybe it was just a silly coincidence. Looking at the clock, she realized that her styling appointment was in just a few minutes. She arrived at the salon just in time.

CHAPTER 11

The eclectic salon was modest, exactly what she needed. The owner was working at the front, by one of the styling chairs. He was sweeping up after his last client. The man appeared to be in his mid thirties. His strong build and deep voice was complimented by a surprising grace and subtle feminine charms. Long, golden cornrows cascaded over his shoulders and down his back. He smiled as Katie neared the front register to check in.

He motioned for her to come on in and take a seat wherever she would like. Five chairs were available. His afternoon crowd was not due for a couple hours. A variety of paintings adorned the walls. She noticed several abstracts, a few Andy Warholesque things. There were a couple of paintings she recognized as old hip-hop legends.

"Hi. I'm Jamal and I'll be taking care of you this morning."

His tall, muscular body moved like a dancer's as he made his way over to her.

"Is this your first time in my salon?"

"Yes. It's been awhile since I've had my hair done," she replied somewhat nervously.

"Have a seat, sweetie. Let me get you a little duster. I'll be right back."

He gracefully made his way to the supply shelf and returned with a shiny, hot pink apron draped over his broad shoulder. Tiny white polka dots covered its surface. He gently placed it over her head while turning her in front of the mirror. Katie gazed at her reflection, once again surprised by her glowing complexion. She decided to try something a little more daring than usual.

"I was thinking about going red," she said tentatively.

A smile spread across his face as he replied, "Oh I'm loving it! You just sit back and let me work my magic."

Jamal sprayed her hair with several pumps of water and combed through her generous locks. He took his time brushing it out and giving her a professional trim. The absence of gray hair was a pleasant surprise. Normally her gray roots were making an unpleasant appearance throughout her hair. Maybe the sun was helping to fade them out. There had been a considerable amount of sunny days since she had left the city.

Jamal parted Katie's hair and worked out her cut section by section. He went in the back for a few moments and returned with a generous mixture of color.

"You've been blessed with gorgeous curls. Oh yes. This is going to add a little depth. It's hard to improve with your natural color," he added.

She smiled at the compliments, imagining he did this with all of his clients, yet it did not stop her from enjoying the attention. His strong hands were surprisingly gentle as he applied the dye and folded the foil wraps on each portion. The fumes were pleasantly mild compared to treatments she'd received in the past. The aroma had hints of incense and spice. He guided her over to the blow-drying chair and placed the headpiece over her hair. She relaxed with a gossip magazine as the dye worked its magic. Forty minutes later the bell sounded and she was escorted to the sink. She leaned her head back to the washbowl. Warm water rinsed the thick solution from her hair. Bright, crimson dye swirled lazily down the sink.

Jamal took his time, gently massaging her scalp, temples, and the nape of her neck. The attention was absolutely divine. She was beginning to drift off as he carefully wrapped a towel around her head. He led her back to the chair turning her away from the mirror. He spent his time combing out the damp curls. After awhile, he stopped, carefully regarding his work. With a coy tilt of the head, a smile brightened his face.

"You ready, Katie?"

She looked up with excited anticipation. He slowly turned her around until she was facing the mirror. For a moment, all she could do was stare. Katie's flowing locks had been turned into a rich, scarlet masterpiece. Subtle highlights had been strategically placed throughout her hair. The rich color brought out the deep green of her eyes, while making her skin resemble a porcelain doll. She tried to find the words and was at a loss. *My God*, she thought, *I look twenty years younger*. Katie rose slowly out of her chair and faced Jamal. Tears welled in her eyes, threatening to spill down her face. She rushed over and gave her new stylist a hug. He hugged her right back.

"All right, baby girl. You come back in about two months for a touch up."

"I definitely will!"

Jamal led her back to the register and penciled her in for another appointment. She paid her bill and added a generous tip. As she walked to her car, she caught the eyes of several shoppers.

Katie decided to make one more stop before heading home. She drove a few more blocks down Main Street and discovered the Wednesday afternoon farmers' market. A couple dozen tents lined the street. Farmers and food vendors were selling produce, flowers, and delicious gourmet food. Walnut trees lined the sidewalk. The tree's leaves were colored brilliantly with scarlet reds, deep orange, and yellow. Fall was working its magic on the canopy. Their vibrant foliage cascaded down the branches. Vivid colors of autumn were seen under the market tents. Gold and orange chrysanthemums were displayed in front of the flower vendor's tent. Their colorful petals caught the light of the afternoon sun. Red, yellow, and orange bell peppers filled the wooden crates of an organic vendor's tent. Their skin glowed like rich orbs in the soft sunlight. Several of the produce tables displayed pumpkins.

She headed to the information tent and was pleased to see the market manager chatting with some of the local vendors. She introduced herself. A tall, slender woman in her late forties greeted Katie with a smile. Her face was tan from working outside. She wore a pair of loose fitting jeans and a worn denim jacket. Her light brown hair was tied in a ponytail under her 49ers baseball cap. Her hazel eyes were alert, clear. Jane Davidson reached out warmly and shook her hand.

"Katie, it's wonderful to see you again! How was the move?" she asked.

"Everything went really well. I should have all of my plants ready by March. The greenhouse and nursery supplies are being delivered tomorrow," she answered enthusiastically.

They chatted about the market, and Katie watched the interactions of the vendors with their customers. It was evident that there were many local patrons. The friendly transactions were easy and cheerful. Her heart was filled with excitement and anticipation at the thought of starting her new market. It was going to be just perfect.

Before leaving, the manager introduced Katie to several vendors. They welcomed her to the market. This would soon be her new family. She tried to remember their names as she made her way down the rows of tents. There were several fruit and vegetable vendors, flowers, honey, eggs, and craft tents. It would take her a while to get to know each of them. She had been lucky in developing friendships over the years working with the farming community. Farmers tended to support one another. They were a tight group. She looked forward to the new friendships.

She decided to stop by the flower stand before leaving the market. A petite, elderly woman named Margaret, introduced herself and encouraged Katie to pick out her favorite flowers. She chose a bouquet of deep yellow and orange chrysanthemums. The woman refused Katie's money but agreed to try some of her potted herbs in the spring.

"Do you ever grow Feverfew plants, dear?" Margaret asked.

"I actually do. I'll make sure to plant some up on Friday," Katie answered.

"That'd be wonderful."

Margaret carefully wrapped the flowers in a shiny sheet of orange plastic wrap. She tied the bouquet with a small yellow ribbon. Katie noticed her fingers were twisted and deformed. Her hands shook as she handed her the bouquet.

After saying her goodbyes to the flower vendor, she made her way over to one of the organic vegetable stands. The owners, Eric and Julie Blackwell, were a young married couple in their mid twenties. She spent some time admiring the produce and making small talk. She paid for her vegetables and two large pumpkins. Eric helped her carry the purchases back to her jeep. Once her vehicle was loaded with her favorite fall produce and flowers, she happily made her way back to the cabin filled with excitement over her upcoming market.

Parking in her driveway, Katie grabbed her pumpkins one by one and carried them over to the wooden porch swing. She placed them on each side. After admiring them, she went back to the car. As she turned, she was startled to see her familiar goose sitting in front of one of the new pumpkins. He was nibbling away at the shiny skin, and he honked loudly as she gazed in his direction.

"Hello, little boy. Are you ready for some dinner?" He honked enthusiastically.

"Ok sweetie, I'll be right back."

Katie let herself into the cabin. She walked to the sink and searched underneath. She retrieved a crystal vase and filled it with warm water. She took out her chrysanthemum bouquet and cut the ends off the stems and placed them in the vase. She put the flowers on top of the kitchen table by the window. She took the fresh vegetables and made a large salad, and divided the dinner into a large salad bowl and a smaller Tupper Ware container.

The goose was waiting patiently outside for his dinner. She placed the bowl and large container of water alongside it. He eyed her softly and honked in approval. She drizzled some Italian dressing on her salad and poured herself a glass of Chardonnay. She came back on the deck and sat down in the cedar porch swing. The two of them ate their salad and enjoyed the beautiful woods.

Later that evening, she watched some television. A reality show was on. Her eyes were growing heavy as the wealthy women screamed at one other in a fancy French restaurant. Glasses of wine were being thrown about. The fight had something to do with one of the housewives being excluded from a party. Katie could not keep her eyes open. She sat up and turned off the television. She fell asleep soon after. If there were dreams of angels or meadows, she couldn't remember them.

CHAPTER 12

Camellia called the next morning and invited her to join the family for Sunday Mass. She accepted eagerly. A few minutes after the call, the sound of a car horn in the driveway echoed through the woods. Katie heard the Berry brothers' van pull up as she was finishing her second cup of coffee. The boys opened their doors simultaneously and headed over to the cabin. She greeted them at the doorstep with a smile.

"You can pull into to the open field." She pointed to the large clearing behind the cabin. "I was thinking about setting up the greenhouse away from the trees. The trailer can go at the side of the cabin. I'll bring out some coffee and meet you in the field."

"Thank you, Katie," the brothers responded in unison.

The boys began the work of moving her nursery supplies out of the van. As with their last visit, they patiently waited for her instructions. They worked together carrying large sections of the greenhouse into the open field. They assembled the pieces surprisingly quickly.

They unloaded several dozen bags of soil, seeds, potting containers, and planting supplies. Large containers of seeds, soil and tools were moved back into the back shed while others were placed inside the greenhouse. Soon they were sharing stories of college life. She was surprised at how quickly the time went with their engaging tales of fellow students and classroom studies. Their positive energy was contagious.

After spending several hours together, in pleasant company, Katie paid them in cash and added a generous tip.

"I can't thank you enough for all of your hard work."

"Katie, I think that the country suits you. You look absolutely beautiful," Paul added shyly.

"Thank you so much. I really love it out here."

"It shows," Ted added smiling.

"Give us a call if you need any more help."

"You'll be the first ones I call," she answered. "Now, you boys enjoy the rest of your afternoon!"

They waved back from the van as they made their way down the hill.

Katie took a deep breath and felt her excitement stirring. This feeling always surfaced at the beginning of a new growing season. She decided to start the new sweet peas and herb starts this afternoon. The recycled containers were soon lined up on a large potting bench next to the greenhouse. She opened a bag and reached her small hands into the rich, organic soil. The earthy aroma was soothing. Slowly and methodically she filled pot after pot with soil and seeds. She labeled each container with its variety and a brief description. She made sure to plant a few pots of Feverfew seeds. This plant could be very beneficial for her new friend, Margaret, at the farmers' market. The herb was helpful in easing the pain of arthritis. She would make sure to give her several plants.

After a gentle spray of water, she moved them into the greenhouse. Several hours went by. Planting was a form of meditation that she relished. The sun began to set just as she was finishing her last batch of herbs. She placed the tray of seeded containers in the greenhouse and closed the door. She noticed that it had already warmed up considerably in the afternoon sun. She headed back to her cabin feeling content with her hard day's work. She turned in early that evening. The next day would be a marathon of planting and soil preparation. Sunday would be her day to rest. She looked forward to it with anticipation.

CHAPTER 13

The Sanchez family arrived at Katie's cabin mid morning. They offered to drive her to church. After Mass, she would join them for Sunday dinner. She invited Camellia and Steven inside while the children hunted for the goose. Camellia's husband offered to take a quick look at the bedroom ceiling. He studied the varnished paint job for a few moments and asked if he could borrow a ladder. He went back outside to survey the property. After several moments he came back looking somewhat perplexed.

"Katie, I'm afraid that the space above your bedroom ceiling isn't big enough for an attic. The roof lines up with the cross beams of the cabin just above your bedroom. There might be some insulation above but not much else. That's probably the extent of it. As far as the varnish goes, it really doesn't make much sense. Whoever applied it wasn't very familiar with home improvement projects at all. There may have been some slight cracking in the beams from seismic shifts in the ground. It would've been a much better idea to apply some fiberglass mesh tape, and some drywall depending on the severity of the damage. It could've easily been sanded down. But the varnish is a temporary fix. It's just a matter of time before the cracks reappear."

Katie was disappointed to hear the news. It would have been nice to have the extra attic space for her antique collections. She realized that she would either have to hire someone to repair her ceiling or find the time to do it herself. It was another home improvement project to add to her growing list. This was one of the sacrifices of home ownership.

"On the plus side, I did call my friend Daryl who works with the home security firm my wife told you about. He was able to work out a deal on a security package for your home if you're interested." Steven remarked.

"Wonderful. That'd be great," Katie answered.

"Perfect. I'll give him a call this week to set it up."

The family piled into the back of their white mini van and made their way to church. Saint Brigid Catholic Church was a modest building. Colorful stain glass windows adorned the sides of the cathedral. The Stations of the Cross were beautifully depicted within the detailed images.

The family blessed themselves with holy water before entering the church. Katie followed the family to their seats and quietly kneeled before making her way down the aisle. The aroma of candles filled the room. Katie noticed a large statue of Saint Brigid in the corner of the church. This happened to be her patron saint that she had chosen for her Confirmation name many years ago.

Saint Brigid is best remembered for her charity work, spiritualism, and protector of women. She founded a famous school of art in Kildare, Ireland. Her illuminated manuscripts were known to be some of the most beautiful in the world. It was one more sign that she was in the perfect place in life.

The congregation rose from their seats and joined along with the choir as they sang the entrance procession song. A nice looking teenage boy, dressed in white robes, carried a large, gold Crucifix down the center aisle. His face was rigid with concentration as he made his way toward the altar. Lizzie smiled as he passed their pew. He was followed with several altar servers, as well as three children dressed in white. A small, elderly priest named Father Peter followed slowly behind. Little Bennie's face lit up when he saw the priest. Mass began and the young children were soon called up to attend Sunday Bible School. Bennie ran as fast as he could to the front of the church to join the class. Father Peter gently patted Bennie on the shoulder.

"We have one more lamb to add to our flock today. Good lad," he added.

The congregation laughed quietly. Camellia put her hand over her eyes and appeared to be positively mortified by the entire scene. Katie gave her a reassuring smile. The church choir sang aloud as the children made their way back down the aisle. Their Sunday school teacher, a middle aged, heavyset woman, proudly led them outside to their morning teachings. Bennie waved to his family as he walked by their pew.

The mass continued with the readings. Father Peter announced the Gospel of Mathew, Chapter 18.1-5,10. He read aloud in a clear, gentle voice:

The disciples approached Jesus and said,

"Who is the greatest in the Kingdom of heaven?"

He called a child over, placed it in their midst, and said,

"Amen, I say to you, unless you turn and become like children,

you will not enter the Kingdom of heaven.

Whoever humbles himself like this child

Is the greatest in the Kingdom of heaven.

And whoever receives one child such as this in my name receives me.

"See that you do not despise one of these little ones,

for I say to you that their angels in heaven

always look upon the face of my heavenly Father."

The elderly priest focused his homily on the life of Jesus and his great love of children. He encouraged his parish community to treat all young people with kindness, compassion, and understanding as Jesus had instructed. He explained the importance of opening one's heart and soul like a child in order to draw closer to God.

Katie was impressed with the Father's gentleness of spirit. After Mass, the family made their way outside and introduced Katie to Father Peter Deane. The elderly priest smiled. Taking her hand in his, he regarded her with a certain gracefulness.

"Do I detect a touch of the Irish in those green eyes?"

"You do indeed," she laughed.

He inquired about her Irish heritage and enthusiastically acknowledged that he was indeed familiar with several members of the O'Brien clan of Galway. His baby blue eyes softened as he remembered his beloved country. After introductions, the family said their goodbyes to their friends in the parish and slowly made their way over to the van.

Katie noticed that Lizzie continued to look back over her shoulder in the direction of the church. Her attention seemed to be directed at the young altar server that had carried the processional cross during Mass. The boy waved to Lizzie and she waved back. Her mother witnessed the flirtation and pretended not to notice. Camellia's eldest daughter could not stop smiling during the entire ride back to the house.

CHAPTER 14

They arrived at the Sanchez's home at noon. The ladies headed over to the kitchen to get their meal started. Bennie and his father hurried back to the bedrooms to change into their 49ers shirts. The little boy ran back to the kitchen after getting dressed to show off his red and gold jersey.

"Me and daddy are going to watch the Forty Niners, Katie!"

"Bennie, would you do me a big favor? Will you let me know if they make a touchdown?"

His eyes grew large with excitement. "Yes, I will tells you when they make their touchdowns. They are going to win today."

Steven walked up and put a hand on his small shoulder. He looked proudly at his son.

"That's good to hear. He gets it right every time. I think I may let him choose my football picks this year."

"Oh no he won't," Camellia interrupted. "I don't want my son gambling before kindergarten."

"Yes dear," he smiled mischievously at her.

Lizzie turned on the kitchen radio and found her station. The top ten hits of the week were being counted down. Taylor Swift was next. Katie had to admit that her new song was catchy. Camellia patiently let the girls in on the secrets of creating the perfect marinara sauce. One of Katie's jobs was to cut up the fresh herbs for the sauce. Camellia retrieved several ceramic bowls containing fresh herbs. As Katie cut up the sage, basil, thyme, and fresh scallion, she had an overwhelming feeling of Déjà vu.

Soon, the delicious aroma of fresh garlic, sage, olive oil, and tomato sauce filled the beautiful home. Camellia poured a generous glass of Cabernet for herself and Katie.

"Cooking is always more enjoyable with wine," she laughed.

"If I had known that was the secret, I'd have tried to learned to cook years ago," Katie replied.

After simmering the sauce, making a generous salad, and baking the garlic bread, the daughters set the table while the women took turns bringing the dishes out to the formal dining room. Steven and his son cheered and hollered from the living room. Bennie suddenly burst into the kitchen yelling,

"The Niners made a touchdown, Katie!! Woo Hoo!!"

Katie cheered with excitement. She gave Bennie a quick high five.

Camellia called her husband to the table for lunch. They took their seats in the formal dining room. A framed painting of *The Last Supper* hung on the wall behind Steven. The family joined hands with one another and bowed their heads. Little Bennie smiled down at his plate as he shyly held Katie's hand.

"Would you say grace, my love?" Camellia asked of her husband.

"Of course."

After the prayer, Camellia looked up at her husband as he took her hand and gently kissed it. The family passed around the bowls of pasta, bread, and salad. Conversation died, and everyone began eating. Steven broke the silence by raising his glass to toast. "To the amazing chefs that prepared this wonderful feast, you've outdone yourselves today!"

The women thanked him and the family took turns toasting. Bennie giggled as he clinked his glass of milk against Katie's wine glass. She smiled at him warmly. The little boy was just about the cutest thing she had ever seen. Bugsy, the Golden Retriever, thumped his tail against the marble floor every time Bennie dropped a piece of his lunch on the floor.

As the family continued to make light conversation with one another, Katie noticed that Lizzie kept looking down at her phone on her lap. Her little sister quickly caught on and started giggling with her hands over her mouth.

"Lizzie has a boyfriend," she squealed.

Her big sister shot her a cold look, and told her to mind her own business, "You don't know what you're talking about, little brat!"

Lizzie blushed and stared down at her plate.

"Stop teasing your sister. Lizzie, put your phone away and quit calling Jessie names. You know the rules," Camellia quipped.

Steven set his fork down on the table and placed his hands together.

"What's this I'm hearing about my eldest daughter having a boyfriend? It's impossible since my little girl is way too young to be dating. Then again," he quipped, "perhaps it'd be a nice idea to have this mystery boy over to the house."

"Really dad?"

Her father answered her with a big smile.

"Well, I was just polishing up the rifle collection this morning, it might be nice to test them out."

"Dad, No!" Lizzie wailed.

Camellia shot her husband an exasperated look and quickly turned the conversation to Halloween. She asked what the children were planning to dress up as this year. Lizzie looked up at her mother in relief as Camellia cleverly steered the subject away from her love life. The children eagerly discussed costume ideas and talked over one other as they bragged about the enormous candy collection they would find.

Katie explained that Halloween was one of her favorite holidays. The children questioned her at length about her Halloween decorations, and whether she would be dressing up. Bennie demanded that she must join them in trick- or-treating. The family agreed that it was a wonderful idea. She happily accepted their offer.

After the table was cleared and the dishes were put away, the family gathered around the piano to sing some songs. Katie warned them all that she could not carry a tune. They took turns encouraging her to join them. Bennie looked up at her with excitement. She finally gave into their requests and the family began to sing. Everyone was asked to pick a favorite song. Steven suggested they start with *Brown Eyed Girl*. He gave his wife a quick wink during he chorus. They all raised their voices and sang. Bennie and Lizzie held hands and danced around the piano. Bennie did not know the words to the song and so just murmured "la la la la" while running in circles. He eventually became dizzy and collapsed on the floor giggling.

Then it was Katie's turn to choose a song. She thought of her selection nervously. "Would you by any chance know the words to *Danny Boy*?"

The family looked at one another and smiled.

"I think he has the prefect voice for this one," Camellia replied, nodding in the direction of Steve.

They pulled up their chairs close to the piano as Steven sang in a beautiful tenor voice.

> "Oh Danny boy, the pipes, the pipes are calling
>
> From glen to glen, and down the mountain side
>
> The summer's gone, and all the flowers are dying
>
> 'Tis you, 'tis you must go and I must bide.
>
> But come ye back when summer is in the meadow
>
> Or when the valley's hushed and white with snow
>
> 'Tis I'll be here in sunshine or in shadow
>
> Oh Danny boy, oh Danny boy, I love you so..."

By the end of the song Katie's eyes were brimming with tears. She collected herself when she realized everyone was staring.

"Sorry, it gets me every time. Steven, you have a wonderful voice."

He gave a modest smile as the family clapped and demanded he take a bow.

CHAPTER 15

Katie's neighbors dropped her at the cabin in the late afternoon. Bennie smiled and waved goodbye from the back of the van as they drove away. She decided to take a quick detour to the shed before heading into the cabin. After several minutes of searching, she located five orange and black storage containers. She picked one up and headed to the house. The white gander was sitting between the porch rocker and the new pumpkins.

"Hello Mr. Goose, are you nice and cozy on my porch?"

He honked loudly in response. She smiled down at the friendly goose and admired his relaxed attitude.

"I guess it's about time that I choose a name for you. Let me think…well, you seem like a cozy, little boy. How about we call you *Cozy*?"

The goose honked eagerly back at her.

"Alright then, Cozy it is. Now you relax, while I move these Halloween decorations," she smiled.

One by one, she carried the storage containers back to her cabin. A cool breeze blew against her face and hair. The warm sunshine slowly disappeared as dark clouds took its place. She brought the boxes into the living room and gently pulled out the treasures inside. Each antique was wrapped in tissue paper. Katie had a collection of vintage Halloween decorations that she'd collected over the years. As she organized the pieces, the wind began to gather strength outside the cabin. The windows shook from fierce gusts. She sorted through the black cats, witches, pumpkins, ghosts, and skeletons. Carefully, she distributed her favorite pieces throughout the cabin. A couple hours later, her rustic home was Halloween-ready. She looked forward to having the children over to enjoy her decorations.

The cabin was particularly cold that evening. She decided to head back to her bedroom and cuddle up with a book. Katie climbed into her warm bed and snuggled under the covers. She reached for, *Les Misérables*, which was on top of her bedside table. As she read the beautiful passages of Victor Hugo, she discovered that Marius and Cosette were falling in love in a beautiful French garden. It was one of her favorite parts of the story. After reading for several minutes, she stretched out in bed and plumped up her pillows. Outside, the wind moaned. As she adjusted the covers, something strange caught her attention. There appeared to be several new scratch marks on the varnish of the ceiling. As she tried to make sense of the bizarre streaks, her vision blurred and then darkened. She closed her eyes and when she opened them she knew immediately that she was no longer in her bedroom.

CHAPTER 16

A cottage awaited her in the distance. It was nestled under an enormous oak tree. Little violets filled the flower boxes under the cottage window. A comfortable, wooden swing complimented the white porch. A milk churn sat beside the front door. There was a beautiful pewter cross, which marked the entrance to the home. A young woman approached the cottage in a pony drawn cart. The rhythmic sound of hoof beats echoed down the dirt road. Her dark red hair hung past her shoulders. She wore an old-fashioned dress. It looked homespun. Her old boots rested on the rig board. The memory was hers and it made absolutely no sense. All she could do was watch. The pony eagerly made her way over to the cottage.

"Whoa, Sassy," her driver commanded.

The dapple-gray pony obediently came to a stop in front of the home. Several geese and chickens honked and clucked as they ran by. She unhooked her lead from the buggy and gently guided the small horse to the red barn. The pony trotted alongside the young woman, anticipating its evening meal. After setting the pony in her stall, with a flake of hay and a generous portion of oats, Sassy had put in a long day; she made her way back to her carriage. More than half of her supply of potatoes, turnips, cabbages, and eggs were still in the back rig. A year ago she would have sold out by early afternoon. Today, she was lucky to be rid of a third of it. She gathered her remaining produce and brought it down to the root cellar along with several cartons of chicken and duck eggs. She placed the basket of potatoes on the back shelf. She noticed a strange odor coming from the collection of tubers. It was surprising that she had not noticed it when she had harvested them earlier. She decided to take a couple of the potatoes back to the house with her. She grabbed her basket of herbs and roots from the backboard and headed over to the family cottage.

She found her mother resting in the modest bedroom, quietly reciting the Angelus. She held a Bible on her lap.

"I'm home, ma. How ya feeling?"

"As I said, growing old isn't for sissies, my dear Katie."

She smiled at her mother's quick wit, aware that she was hurting. Always trying to put on a brave face. Her green eyes glistened in the candlelight. The mother's plump, little hands clung to her Bible. Even the slightest touch could bring on the agonies of her relentless arthritis.

Katie quickly took her basket to the kitchen table. She placed the potatoes on a cutting board of the counter. With a sharp knife, she delved deep into the soggy skin and paired the spud in half. A puff of dust and putrid odor filled the air. To her dismay, she realized that the potato was completely black and rotted throughout. She'd noticed several dead vines in the field during the last harvest. There had been no time to investigate since she would be late to market. She had dug up a basket worth and left the rest. Rumors of a possible blight hitting some farms in the neighboring villages had been making its way around town. It would be devastating for her livelihood if the disease spread. She would have to check the crop in the morning when there was more light.

She gathered up the potato remnants and tossed them in the fireplace. She'd have to worry about it later. It was time to get back to business. She sorted through her collection of herbs gathered on the way home from the market. Taking her pestle, she began to grind the pungent leaves into the mortar. A jar of honey was on the dining room table. It was spooned out and added to the mix. Lastly, she added some Feverfew leaves, ground willow bark, and a sprinkle of cinnamon for good measure. Once her salve was ready, Katie quickly took the remedy to the back room. He mother patiently waited for her afternoon treatment. She put a gentle hand on her mother's shoulder and carefully lifted the back of her nightdress. Her arthritis was returning with the cold weather. Her small body appeared twisted and crippled. Katie used all of her knowledge of the local herbs to combat the aggressive disease. Firmly, she massaged the salve onto her mother's back, legs, arms, and finally on her gnarled hands.

"Ah darlin, that is pure Heaven. You do have the touch don't you, my dear."

She smiled lovingly in response to the complement. Since her father's death, the task of running their modest farm had fallen to Katie. Patrick O'Brien had been the rock of their family, always quick to laugh, never complaining about the hard living of tenant farming. A joke and a good story always lingered in his eyes. He was loved by his neighbors and was always ready to get his hands dirty. His sudden heart attack shocked the family. Katie had no choice but to take the reins and attempt to run the farm herself. Her father had taught her everything he knew about planting, keeping poultry, and business management at the market. With no sons,

Katie received all of his instruction and knowledge. The days were long and she often fell asleep before her head even touched her pillow.

Because of her father's kindness and high standing in the community, there were several young men that would come by and take turns plowing the fields and offering their muscle for some of the more difficult chores. Katie hated to take charity and always offered them fresh eggs, milk, and baked goods from the kitchen. They accepted the gifts cheerfully and continued to offer their services. With news of *The Great Hunger* sweeping the country, the local townspeople were slowly leaving the Village of Kinvara. Her market outings brought in smaller amounts of money each day. Rent was due at the beginning of the month. She wondered if they would have enough. The thought of this made a pain in the pit of her stomach.

Katie stoked the fire and heated the kettle. It might be a nice idea to have a little cup and sit out on the front porch. It would be relaxing to watch the sunset before her ma woke from her nap. Soft snoring echoed from the bedroom. Her mother could enjoy a cup of nettle tea after she woke. She removed a small jar from the cupboard. Inside were several dried nettle branches and leaves. She focused intently on her tea preparation and soon became lost in her thoughts. A sudden hard pounding on the door made her jump as she was removing her iron kettle from the fire. She dried her hands on her apron and went to answer the door. To her annoyance, she realized that the landlord's son was standing on the porch.

"Good evening, Katie. I was just in the neighborhood and thought I might drop in for a friendly visit."

The likelihood that he was on his way to the local tavern was a much more realistic scenario. The landlord's son, James Williams, had grown up with Katie in the town of Kinvara. His family had moved from England in order to manage several tenant farms in Galway. Most of her neighbor's landlords still lived across the pond. This was not the case for the Williams family. They enjoyed being hands-on managers.

The boy's life had been one of excess, squander, and frivolity. He wanted for nothing and the result was a young man spoiled by wealth. As she reluctantly let him inside the cottage, he immediately stooped with an exaggerated bow, reaching to take Katie's hand in his. James's lips lingered longer than necessary on her skin. After kissing the top, he turned her hand over and examined the calloused skin. Katie slowly pulled her hand back and tried to keep her face from showing a growing impatience.

"Would you like some tea, Mr. Williams?"

"I've told you many times, Katie: call me James. No need for formality, we've known each other since we were kids, no?"

Her forced smile caused her mouth twitch.

"And yes, tea sounds lovely," he answered with exaggerated formality.

Katie struggled to hide her uneasiness. James had been nothing but forward and presumptuous since her father's passing. This unannounced visit was just one more example of his growing arrogance and entitlement. She lowered the pot and set up two cups and saucers on the table. He pulled out a chair and insisted that she join him. She took her seat reluctantly. The proximity of their chairs made her uneasy. The heavy scent of whiskey permeated the air around him. She poured the tea into two porcelain cups adorned with violets and roses, making sure to leave room for milk.

She took a small pitcher from the icebox and set it next to him on the table. He reached into his right hand pocket and retrieved a small silver flask. She noticed the ornate designs etched along its surface, and imagined that the value of the flask could easily pay her rent for several years.

"Taste, my dear?" he smiled wickedly.

She silently declined his offer.

"Your loss...angel."

He poured a generous amount of whiskey into the cup and took a large swallow.

"You know, Katie, you don't have to struggle as you do."

His arrogant tone annoyed her. James had known only the best schools and tutors in his youth. The educated young man enjoyed using his knowledge as a powerful tool of persuasion when dealing with the tenement farmers. Many of the villagers were intimidated by his formal etiquette, but for Katie, his eagerness to show his superiority made him appear foolish.

"It's a shame to see such a lovely young lady forced to work as hard as you do. Your hands are beginning to look like well," he paused with a look of disgust, "the hands of a washer woman."

He gazed across the table with a look of exaggerated sympathy.

Anger welled in her chest and she found it difficult not to hurl something at his head. Katie shot him a defiant look and cautiously chose her words. She quipped, "Times are hard for everyone. I thank God everyday for the ability to provide for my ma and myself. I praise the Good Lord for the gifts and blessings that we have. A bit of hard work never hurt anyone," she added.

Whatever his intentions were, she did not like where this was heading. James chuckled to himself as if reading her thoughts.

"Don't worry, Ms. Katie. I am not proposing anything indecent."

To her amazement, the young lord suddenly took to one knee and gazed up earnestly.

"My dear, will you do me the honor of being my wife?"

Katie took in a deep breath, before losing her temper. "Mr. Williams, this a great honor, but I am in no way in a position to take your hand in marriage. You are of noble birth, and I am but scraping by, alongside my ma, on our small farm."

He looked up at her scrutinizing her for several minutes.

"Well are you not the charming one, young lass. I have told you many times to call me James. I would have you think long and hard on my proposition. A great famine is spreading in this God forsaken country. Your people will not be surviving long on their potatoes. Don't doubt that this will not wreak havoc on this side of the isle. These foolish villagers will be scattering like rats once all of their crops are destroyed. How do you propose to make your monthly rent if you do not have any customers to sell to at the market?" He smiled cruelly.

"Well, my lord, I will cross that bridge when I find myself on it. God willing. Our lands will be free of the blight in due time."

He smirked at her and stood back up.

"Don't wait too long, my love. My offer may not be so generous in the future."

And with that he grabbed her by the arm and forcibly kissed her mouth, exploring her breasts with his small hands. His awakened manhood was obvious as he pushed roughly against her dress. She stepped back in shock and shot out her hand to slap him as he grabbed it just inches from his face. The sickening taste of his whiskey lingered on her lips.

"Don't be a fool, girl. Believe it when I tell you, I do not give second chances."

His smile quickly disappeared as his mask came off. His eyes were dark and cruel as he quickly dismissed her with a wave of a gloved hand. He stormed to the front door, grabbed the knob, and slammed it behind him.

Katie's fury rose inside her. Tears of anger filled her eyes, threatening to spill over. Her mother called quietly from her bedroom.

"What's wrong, child?"

She tried to regain her composure, brushed the tears from her eyes, and headed into her mother's room. The elderly woman looked tired and pained. She walked to her side, bravely trying to hide her emotions.

"It was nothing ma, I'm sorry I woke you, would you like a cup of nettle tea?"

"Are you sure you're alright, my child? I know that life hasn't been easy on you these past couple of years."

"I'm alright, ma. Just had a long day. I need a good night's rest, maybe a nice stroll in the field."

She poured her mother a cup of tea and gently kissed her on the head. Her soft gray hair smelled of violets. Katie headed outside and felt chilled by the evening air. She wrapped her shawl around her shoulders. Her pet goose was sitting in the field looking in her direction. He waddled up to her as she took her seat. She sat down on her porch swing and looked out at the lush fields. There was so much work to do. She sighed and took a sip of her tea. It was cold from setting too long. She heard hoof beats approaching from the dirt road.

A lean black gelding trotted up to her front gate. Sitting atop it was a tall, muscular young man that she had known her whole life. He let himself down and smiled brightly. The goose honked his displeasure at the handsome youth. The gander enjoyed his alone time with Katie. The young gentleman's clothes were clean and recently pressed. A silver pocket watch dangled from a chain attached to the front of his trousers. The setting sun highlighted the red in his dark, wavy brown hair, making his eyes sparkle like the sea.

"Hello Daniel," she greeted her good friend.

"Good evening, Ms. Katie. He took off his hat as he approached her swing. Are you taking a break from all of your work to appreciate the beautiful sunset this evening?"

She scooted over to make room on the swing.

"Please join me, Daniel."

They had always had a natural way between them. As children, they had been constant playmates. Katie remembered climbing trees and exploring all the secret hideouts in the village of Kinvara with him by her side. The two had had many adventures together over the years. He sat down next to her. His long lean legs stretched out in front of him. He clasped his hands together across his chest and leaned back in the swing. His clean scent reminded her of the woods.

"You know, my dear, they say the sunsets in Africa take your breath away. The colors are rich with scarlet and gold, although I am sure the color could not do justice to your fair locks."

He gave her quick wink and a lopsided smile. Katie blushed hotly at his unexpected compliment.

"Well aren't you the charming one tonight?" she replied. "Africa, you say, now that'd be something to write home to ma about."

"Katie, we're both young and full of spirit. I say we travel the world together."

She giggled at his enthusiasm.

"Alright," she played along, "where are we going first?"

"Well young lass, as I mentioned before, we should start with Africa. I know you have quite the way with the critters. We will see the most amazing creatures on the plains. Lovely zebras will gallop across the vast prairie as lightning roars above their heads. Perhaps I'll sit you on top of the back of one of the powerful beasts and you can go for a ride. Would you like that, Katie?"

"That would be…exciting. How about traveling to Holland?" she implored. "I've always wanted to see their beautiful tulips and lush gardens."

"Your wish is my command. We will even find you a lovely pair of wooden shoes for your pretty feet."

They laughed. His deep voice soothed away her troubles.

"Next stop will be America. We'll travel the frontier and meet many cowboys and Indians."

"Will you protect me from all of the dangers of the Wild West?" Katie asked.

"Of course my lass, nothing will harm a hair on your ginger head," he smiled reassuringly.

"So you are going to be my guardian angel?" she teased.

"I will be whatever you want me to be, my love."

His smile slowly faded. Their eyes locked in quiet passion. He reached forward, gently touching the back of her hair as their lips met. Katie completely lost herself in his embrace. Her body warmed at his touch, awakening to previously unexplored desire. After a moment of complete bliss, the two young lovers smiled openly at one another. Katie nestled into his shoulder as he gently brushed the curls from her forehead. Nightingales cried out in the meadow, announcing the approaching evening.

Behind the great oak tree, in the darkness of shadow, James Williams observed the two lovers in their silence. Hatred and jealousy raged in him. He mounted his horse and cruelly yanked the reins. Rocks and dust scattered as he galloped away.

CHAPTER 17

The days and weeks that followed were full of both joy and pain. The young romance grew and blossomed with each passing day. Daniel had proposed to Katie in the middle of the cherry tree orchard on his property. Her heart was overjoyed, and soon, the entire village had heard the news. The villagers eagerly offered their help planning the wedding. It was a much needed distraction from the harsh reality of the failing crops. They held desperately to any traces of hope or happiness. Meanwhile, the whispering signs of famine lingered in the shadows.

Days drifted by like soft, autumn leaves. As the weather grew colder, Katie often found her mother unresponsive in her room, curled up under the covers. The daily treatments no longer seemed to help as the disease continued to progress. By the end of September, her mother began to fail. She was laid to rest on the first of October. It seemed that the entire village was at attendance on the day of the funeral. Shortly before her passing, her mother had a final gift to bestow on her beloved daughter. One rainy evening, by firelight, Mrs. O'Brien softly requested Katie to sit by her side. She instructed her to open the hope chest at the foot of her bed. A gorgeous ivory wedding dress had been placed inside the cedar box. The beauty of the gown took her daughter's breath away. Her mother had secretly worked over many years to purchase the materials. The lovely gown had been crafted in secret with the hope of giving it to Katie on her wedding day. Her hands ached with each delicate stitch bravely enduring the pain of her advancing arthritis. It was her final gift. Tears rolled down her cheeks as she kissed her mother's face. Mrs. O'Brien insisted that her daughter continue on with her wedding plans. In keeping her word, the date was set for All Hallows Eve.

The matron of Dunguaire Castle approached the grieving daughter on the day of her mother's funeral. Katie had known the wealthy woman since she was a young child. Mrs. O'Brien had sewn some of her finest gowns over the years. She had accompanied her during several of the dress fittings. Both of her parents had been of service to the family over the years. Patrick O'Brien had overseen several renovation projects on the castle. His days were very long between assisting the restoration and running the family farm.

Because of the O'Brien's loyal service to the family, Lady McClain offered to host their wedding reception inside the towering walls of the castle. Presently, the grand building was in a state of disrepair and it was not currently occupied. But, the benevolent matriarch suggested that the grand ballroom would be perfect to host their wedding reception. Katie was touched by the gesture and accepted her offer.

The night before their wedding, Daniel stopped by her cottage. He held a small, velvet jewelry case. With great excitement, Katie opened it. Inside was a polished golden locket.

"This belonged to my ma. I know she would want you to have it."

Inside the locket was a picture of Daniel. She was overjoyed with the thoughtful gift. He took the necklace out and gently placed it around her neck. They kissed and said their goodbyes. As he made his way down the steps, she teasingly warned him, "Don't come back before the wedding, my love. It's bad luck."

"You have my word," he answered.

Afterwards, she went inside to her vanity mirror and admired the beautiful gift. Just as soon as she'd sat down, a loud knocking shook the front door. She laughed and ran to open it.

"Daniel, did you come back so soon?"

She opened the door to find her front porch vacant. Looking down, she noticed a small burlap bag and a bouquet of pink roses.

"You silly man," she giggled to herself.

She lifted the roses and breathed in the fragrant blossoms. Strangely, another less pleasant aroma lingered underneath. Reaching inside the bag, she discovered a cinnamon colored teddy bear. As she held the stuffed animal her smile slowly faded. It reeked of whiskey. A small card was attached to the bouquet of roses. It read:

My dear Ms. Katie,

Please accept these gifts as a symbol of my deep regard for you. You will always hold a very special place in my heart. Let this small token of my affection bring a smile to your lovely face. I look forward to seeing you very soon.

Yours Always,

James

The strange letter gave her an uneasy feeling. Images of their last meeting flooded her memory. She could still feel the grip of his hands on her body and his unwanted advances. The thought made her shudder.

Katie and Daniel McCarthy would be moving to their own farm after the wedding. The McCarthy family owned their land. Daniel's father had gifted a generous parcel of farming property for his son and his new wife. It would be bittersweet for her to leave her childhood home, but by doing so her ties to James would be cut forever. No longer would she have to live in fear of his frightening advances. The strange note was ominous. Heading to the back of the cottage with the package, the trashcan was quickly opened and the items went down into the bin. She headed back inside the cottage to prepare for her big day.

If the young woman had not been busy with preparations, she would have heard the heavy footsteps treading just outside the cottage window. They were followed by the sound of furious hoof beats galloping across the road.

A full harvest moon lit the sky. In its glow, there appeared an old woman dressed in black lace. A shimmering veil covered her head. With her back to the old oak tree, she keened wildly. Her cry was carried by the autumn winds and lost on the wings of the nightingales.

CHAPTER 18

The next day was a whirlwind of excitement and preparations. Many of the local women stopped by to help Katie get ready. Lady McClain assisted the nervous bride with her wedding dress. The kind matriarch did her best to fill her mother's shoes. She was grateful for her kindness.

Locks of auburn curls cascaded softly down her delicate shoulders. Tiny white flowers covered her train and veil. The women fussed over her and smiled happily at the final result. Katie was a vision in white. Her friends and neighbors eventually said their goodbyes and slowly made their way back to the church. Numerous times, they offered her a ride, and yet she insisted on going alone. She wanted a few moments to herself. Their vows would take place at sunset according to their wishes. A large reception of Dunguaire Castle would follow their church service. It would be a childhood dream come true.

The sky was taking on a foreboding quality as she approached the old cemetery. The afternoon light flickered like ruby garnets on the graves. Her faithful pony slowed as they neared the graveyard. She dismounted her buggy and carefully made her way to her mother's grave. She lifted her dress as she walked so it would not drag on the ground. She placed a small bouquet of violets under the Celtic cross. The grand stone had been generously donated by Lady McClain and her family.

"I know you will be watching from Heaven today, ma and da. I miss you so. Not a day goes by that you are not in my heart and prayers."

Katie prayed silently for her departed parents. Afterwards, she slowly walked back to her pony cart. To her surprise, she realized that someone was holding Sassy's reins. The sunlight was shining in her eyes and it took her a moment to adjust to the glare. As a cloud obscured the sun's rays, she realized that it was James Williams. Intoxicated, he stumbled forward.

"My dear Ms. Katie," he slurred. "I couldn't let you go off and get married without a proper sendoff."

His eyes were filled with lust and fury. She began moving backwards retreating in alarm and fear.

"I have no time for this, Mr. Williams. I need to get back to the church," Katie remarked.

"I told you to call me James, you little hussy!" These words came out in a sharp hiss. He lunged forward, grabbing her by the arm. "It's time for your special wedding present, Katie."

He laughed as he pulled her against his body. She pushed him back.

"Get away from me," she screamed.

James laughed cruelly, forcefully pushing her to the ground. The smell of whiskey was foul on his hot breath. She gazed up at his face in panic as his body weight held her in place.

His eyes narrowed. He grinned down at her terrified face. She realized his intentions and fought with all her strength to get away. In his stupor, he relented, and she was able to free her right hand from his clumsy grip. He continued to gaze at her with pure evil glowing in his mud-colored eyes. Time seemed to stand still. Everything was happening in slow motion. With her free hand, she reached up and clawed at his face. Her nails dug deeply in his skin. He shrieked in pain. The unexpected assault gave her just enough time to free herself and take off running.

Her heart pounded and the sound roared in her ears as she ran. Her dress was heavy, and made her feel like she was running through molasses. She rushed past gravestones, ceramic angels, and Celtic crosses.

Her first thought was to make her way to the church to get help. A shot rang out as a bullet whizzed by her temple. It missed her by inches. She looked over her shoulder and could see James sprawled out on the ground aiming his pistol at her, all the while smiling like a lunatic.

"Sweet Jesus, he's trying to shoot me," she whispered to herself.

She quickly turned and ran in the opposite direction from Saint Brigids, fearing that if he followed her into church he might endanger her friends and family. She imagined that he would be interested in injuring Daniel. Her shoes were slowing her down in the sandy soil. In his drunkenness, James had not yet made it back on his feet. He appeared to be reloading the pistol. She used her considerable lead to stop for a moment and tear off her shoes. Her bare feet would be an advantage for her.

The intoxicated man continued to follow her as he tripped over gravestones, stumbling through the cemetery. If she could just find the path that led to the main road, it would lead her back to the market area of the village. There, she could find the sheriff's office and get help. The ground became harder, with each step was increasingly painful to maneuver. She followed the gravel path and was soon blocked off by a large cobblestone wall. A clearing could be seen several yards away. As she raced toward it, her foot caught under a large root and she violently fell forward, sliding down toward the base of the hill. Her head struck a sharp rock. Streams of blood trickled down the side of her face, soiling her satin bodice. The crimson drops spread as they hit the delicate fabric, creating a chrism diamond pattern on her beautiful wedding dress. The impact made her stagger and lose balance. In her confusion, she turned left instead of right, heading down an unfamiliar trail.

CHAPTER 19

Shortly before Katie had become lost in the woods, her screams had attracted the attention of several members of the wedding party waiting in the little church of Saint Brigid. Daniel followed where he heard the commotion and noticed Katie's buggy parked next to her mother's grave. Alarmed and puzzled, he looked up to see James running through the cemetery in pursuit of his bride. Daniel quickly followed after him. Anger welled up in his chest with every stride. He quickly closed the gap between them while greatly fearing for his fiancé's safety. Reaching the drunken man without even being winded, James stopped in his tracks to face him. He was smiling ear-to-ear while grasping for breath. "Well, if it isn't the lucky groom. I was just giving your little Katie, a warm up before her special night."

Daniel glared at him with mounting shock and fury. "You sick son of a bitch! What have you done with her?"

"Well, my handsome friend, the real question you should be asking is, what am I going to do with you?"

Daniel stared at him not understanding his veiled threat. James brought out his pistol from his holster, aimed it and fired.

The slug tore through his sternum and ribcage, splintering bone and destroying flesh. The impact was immediate and deadly. Daniel fell backwards on the ground. The pain was agonizing but couldn't compare to the realization that he could not save his beloved. His blood poured over his shattered pocket watch. The hands marked five thirty. His time had run out as the crimson sky hovered above as a dark omen. His last thoughts were of his precious Katie and the dreams of their life together. A single tear trailed down his cheek and disappeared into the sand.

CHAPTER 20

Katie was unaware of what had occurred and continued her relentless race through the brambles. Thorns and branches tore at her delicate skin. She tried to ignore the pain and find her way back to town. Despite the circumstances, she was beginning to think she might be successful. The trail was starting to look somewhat familiar. The light dimmed, as the sun set over the horizon. Darkening skies continued to glow an eerie red as if the heavens were on fire. She wondered what the guests at the wedding were thinking about her failing to show up. The thought pained her deeply. She imagined all of the preparations taking place at the castle for the reception to follow. The sounds of footsteps echoed behind her. She realized she was still being tracked.

Her heart raced in her chest. The heavy gown dragged and snagged the ground with each painful step. The sharp cries of ravens echoed in the distance, their shrill voices lamenting the approaching twilight. Jagged stones protruded along the trail. Her bare feet suffered painfully from the brutal terrain. Rich soil began to take on a sandy texture as she neared the shoreline. Daylight faded and washed shadows over the lush landscape. If she could only find her way back to the safety of the main road, back to the village of Kinvara. The aroma of the sea was rich, intoxicating. Woodlands quickly gave way to an open shore. Dark waters raged and heaved against the rising tide. Rock cliffs on both sides surrounded her. She had followed the wrong path.

The icy water rolled toward her as she slowed at the sandy bank. With resignation, she watched the churning waves of Galway Bay. Dunguaire Castle appeared like a phantom beacon on the foggy haze. Dim lights glowed in the windows of the grand building. Cold ripples drifted over her battered feet. The water was salty and harsh on her open wounds. Taking a deep breath, while embracing the pain, she made the sign of the cross and whispered a silent prayer to Jesus and the Mother Mary. Heavy footsteps made their way toward her. Inhaling the aroma of the overlapping waves calmed her mind. He stood directly behind her in silence. The young woman held her ground. Rough hands encircled her delicate neck. Her locket ripped from her throat as she was pulled under the frigid water. It floated away on the currents. Her last thoughts were of Daniel.

CHAPTER 21

Slowly, the images broke apart and dissolved into the mist. Katie realized she was lying on her bed gazing up at the ceiling. Tears rolled down her face at memories long since forgotten. Her past life had been revealed to her in every beautiful and agonizing detail. She remembered her love for Daniel and longed for his touch.

Overwhelmed, she told herself that she desperately needed to make sense of it all. She was vaguely aware of the storm, which was gathering outside her cabin. Leaving the warmth of her bed, she went into the kitchen and retrieved a bottle of cold Chardonnay from the refrigerator. Pouring herself a generous glass, she headed into her bathroom. She found a couple of lavender candles and placed them around the claw-foot tub. She wanted to make sure that she had a back up if she lost power.

With trembling hands she started the water. Soft candlelight sent shadows dancing around the wall next to the porcelain tub. She switched off the facet just as the liquid was nearing the surface, slipping off her pajamas and dipping her bare feet in the warm water. She slid inside the bath and was instantly soothed by the scent of lavender oil. Submerging herself in the soapy liquid, her heart and mind raced. Raindrops gently fell on the beams of the old cabin. The wind whipped and moaned in a frenzied uproar just outside her bathroom window. An exceptionally strong downpour was on its way.

She reached over and grabbed her Chardonnay. The cool liquid eased her tongue as she inhaled the fresh hints of pear and apple. She set her glass down on a small table next to the tub. Slowly, she exhaled and attempted to collect her thoughts. The faint whispers of the past echoed in her mind. Deep, muffled voices seemed to come from the walls. The whispering rolled over one another and took on urgency as the raging storm grew in strength. An elderly woman with a rich Irish accent called her by name.

"Katie, come child, sit and have a cup of tea with your ma."

The voice slowly changed to the deep and gentle tone of her beloved Daniel.

"They say the sunsets in Africa take your breath away."

And finally, a chilling British voice cried out in the night, "Believe it when I say, I don't give second chances!" This was followed by the slamming of the door.

The wind howled furiously outside, shaking the beams of the cabin as rain pounded against the window. A blast of cold air chilled her skin, sending goose bumps down her arms and back. The lights of the cabin flickered and eventually went out all together. The flames of the candles rose several inches. They were the only source of light as she found herself surrounded by complete darkness. The sound of labored breathing began to radiate from the walls. It became louder and shook the cabin with its steady rhythm.

A dark form emerged from the far corner of the bathroom. It rose from the floor and stretched out to the ceiling. Cold gray mist swirled around its silhouette. A primitive terror seized Katie like a heavy blanket. The whispers from the walls rose in pitch and intensity. She stared in horror and helplessness at the dark figure. The shadowy creature solidified, taking on a human shape. It appeared to be a medium-built man dressed in old-fashioned breeches and a dark navy topcoat. His dirty blond hair and muddy brown eyes materialized with startling detail. With abject terror, she realized that she was looking into the face of James Williams. His dark soulless eyes pierced through her. The smoky image slowly took on a solid form as he stood against the wall looking down on her trembling body. Its shape began to blur as hot steam arose from his flesh. His dark, soulless eyes glowed like two red embers as the corners of his mouth turned upwards in a grin. The specter's teeth grew needle sharp. His legs stretched out grotesquely before him. The breeches ripped, as his leg muscles elongated until they changed into the back of a goat's hindquarters. His hooves scratched and slipped on the hardwood floor. The skin on his face pulled and stretched until it split, tearing to reveal cartridge underneath.

Katie could see the muscles and veins pulse under its thinning skin in detail. Ram-like horns began to emerge from the top of his skull ripping patches of hair and flesh as they slowly rose to the surface. Streams of blood and gore rolled down from the torn and battered flesh and dripped to the floor. It appeared dark and steaming. The pungent smell of rotting flesh filled the air. The demonic creature attempted to communicate in its gravelly voice,

"I've come back for you, Katie."

His mouth opened impossibly wide, simultaneously laughing and shrieking in agony.

"We have unfinished business, you and I. It's time for your special wedding gift that I promised so long ago."

Razor-like talons emerged from his fingertips bridging out towards her. His smile stretched until it wrapped around to the back of his ears. Dark clots of congealed blood dripped from the corners of his upturned mouth. Fragments of its skull and jaw could be seen underneath the torn flesh. The whispering voices of the walls began to overlap and rise to a fever pitch.

"You forgot my gift that I left outside your window, my dear."

He reached behind his back and retrieved the soiled stuffed animal. It appeared to be moving as a multitude of flies covered the creature's face and body. Swollen, white larva crawled over its rotting fur. Maggots lazily rolled off the ginger colored bear and dropped to the floor. The buzzing sound filled the room until she thought her mind would shatter from the insanity of it all. It was in this moment that Katie finally found her voice. Her screams joined the chorus of voices inside the cabin walls as the demon slowly made its way over to the bathtub.

CHAPTER 22

All at once the room shone with a bright spectrum of light as the sound of beating wings filled the air. An angel blocked the creature's path as it made its way towards her. He lifted a Crucifix and held it at the demon. Katie immediately recognized the cross as the one that had rested above her ancestral home in Ireland.

"Get out demon! In the name of the Father, the Son, and the Holy Spirit! Go back to the Hell from which you came from!"

The creature shrieked as if it was being burned and quickly backed away. Its hooves scratched and slipped on the floor. Black smoke smoldered off its skin as it began to peel away and drip. A putrid rotting smell drifted from its flesh, and suddenly it was no more.

Katie tried to gasp for breath as her guardian averted his eyes for the sake of modesty.

"My dear, you best be getting dressed. I will be waiting for you outside."

He quietly walked out of the room. Her heart pounded in anticipation as she quickly dried off and changed into a pair of pink flannel pajamas. She was overcome with raw emotion. Slowly making her way toward her protector, she stopped for a moment and gazed at him from the doorway.

Her eyes filled with tears.

"Daniel?" she whispered quietly.

"Hello, my love. Do you remember me now?"

She tentatively reached her hand up and touched his face. He closed his eyes as her slender fingers traced his skin.

"How could I have ever forgotten," she replied as a tear rolled down her cheek.

He reached down and tenderly wiped it away. He drew her close as they passionately embraced one another. Time and space no longer existed for them.

Several moments later, they stepped back and lovingly regarded one another.

"We have much to talk about, my love. Would you come with me?" he asked gently.

"I will."

He took her hand and embraced her body against his broad chest as his wings spread out gloriously. In a moment they were back in a meadow of tulips standing in a vast orchard of cherry trees. Thunder rolled in the distance and the storm clouds swelled with precipitation. Daniel took her by the hand and led her under the shelter of the cherry trees. He eased her down at the base of a large tree stump. He paced back and forth for a few moments. After gathering his thoughts, he began to speak.

"In our past life together, I failed to save you."

His face grew tense and his eyes were deep with pain and regret.

"Sometimes we are given a choice in the afterlife. I chose to come back in the form of your guardian. I have been by your side since the day you took your first breath in this new life. I have tried to protect you with the powers that I have been gifted. But, there are rules that must be followed. I have been able to watch and assist you to the best of my abilities. I could not allow you to see my physical state. My job hasn't been easy, my love. You have made some interesting choices and protecting you has been challenging," he chuckled softly.

Katie blushed at the thought of him seeing her life playing out. Her mind tried to wrap itself around the idea that he had been watching over her since the day she was born. There were many moments in her journey that she would gladly change if she could. Her choices had not always been logical or prudent.

Yet, she knew in the deepest realms of her heart and soul that he had always been nearby. There had been dangers and many close calls as the years unfolded. Her dreams whispered Daniel's name teasing her with the long forgotten memories. His spirit was always there, and yet, with each waking dawn, his shadow disappeared and life's mundane rituals took center stage. Only in her dreams could she see him once again. In the whisper of the wind or the color of the sunset, he was always there.

"But what has changed? I can see you now." She looked to him in confusion.

"My dear, the rules have changed. The moment you stepped inside your new home, our destinies changed forever. I assume that you have noticed the strange markings above your bed? Your ceiling contains a portal. The previous owners attempted to cover it up. The doorway opened to the realm of light and darkness. It allowed me to step through to your material plane. This is why you can see my physical form. He looked over the plains of tulips and rolling meadows. Our dreams and memories created this place. You are safe here."

Katie smiled brightly as he explained himself. This must mean that they could finally be together after all their time apart. Yet she was confused by his serious brooding expression that was darkening his beautiful face.

"What's wrong, Daniel?" she asked gently.

He looked deep into her eyes as she read his sorrow and pain.

"I'm not the only one that has access to the portal, my love. I'm afraid that what you witnessed tonight was in fact the face of true evil. You must never allow it to take you through the portal. My powers can only protect you on the side of light. If he brings you to his domain, I may not be able to help you. As long as this evil presence is nearby, I can take steps to intercede. But I don't know how long the portal will stay open. Once it's closed, you will no longer be able to see or feel me."

"No. I've waited too long for you to come back to me!"

"I know, Katie. I don't like it either. But I must take steps to protect you while I can. I don't know how much time that we have left together."

His words left her with a feeling of desperation and panic.

"I want you to stay with me tonight. I can't bear to be without you for another moment!"

He embraced her tightly. His lips explored her delicate shoulders as his teeth grazed gently over her softy ivory neck. Daniel pulled her body firmly against his strong lean form. Her desire for him was urgent and deep.

"Please stay with me," she beseeched him.

"Oh my love, I want nothing more than to stay with you forever." He whispered in her ear. "I'm afraid that the rules forbid this," he said sadly.

Then he appeared to gather himself, inhaling deeply. He reached down slowly and lifted her small hands to his lips. He gently kissed the inside of her palms. The sensation sent shivers down her body. He backed away. Taking both of her hands in his, he quietly asked:

"Close your eyes Katie. Please trust me, my love. I promise to keep you safe."

CHAPTER 23

By the time Katie opened her eyes, she was back in her bed with the warm morning sun beating against her window. The night's storm had passed. She slowly sat up feeling tired and worn out. The fact that Daniel was no longer by her side filled her with a deep sense of longing. She wanted nothing more than to wake up in his strong, protective embrace. Her love and desire was beyond anything she had experienced in her life. She wondered if he could see her now. How did the rules work exactly? She sighed deeply and took a breath. There really was no use in agonizing over it. Reluctantly, she climbed out of bed and tried to start her day the best she could.

She had plans to meet with Camellia to visit one of the local wineries. It would be a welcomed distraction from the emotional ride of the night before. Her warm shower eased her tired mind and body. Slipping on a terry cloth robe, she made her way over to her wardrobe. After considering several possibilities, she ended up choosing a white pleated shirt that flowed gracefully toward her knees. She paired it with a form fitting satin blouse that showed off her tiny waist. The green satin brought out the vivid emerald highlights in her eyes. A matching pair of green pumps complimented the curves of her calves. She combed out her loose curls. Red waves spiraled down her shoulders. After applying a light application of makeup, she chose a comb with pearl accents and drew back her flowing hair. A touch of deep mauve lipstick completed the look. Her bright and cheerful appearance masked the turmoil raging in her heart.

The Sanchez family picked Katie up on their way to school. The plan was for Steven to drop them off at the winery for brunch, and then a tour of the vineyards, and their own private wine tasting. It would be a daylong adventure. Camellia's husband planned the day trip as an early birthday present for his wife. He would pick them up later in the afternoon as their designated driver, following their wine tasting adventures.

"Katie, you look like a movie star this morning!" Camellia eagerly called out to her friend.

"Thank you! You look lovely as well," she answered back.

She admired Camellia's pretty white dress. Bright red cherry designs were patterned throughout the soft material. A pair of red heels completed her outfit.

The children smiled as she made her way into the van. The girls talked over one another trying to explain their dramatic school life. Katie was soon caught up on all of the gossip surrounding their teachers, classes, and fellow students. They groaned dramatically as the van pulled up outside their school. Camellia's daughters talked animatedly as they walked toward the campus.

The ride to the vineyard was memorable. They passed miles of farm country. Horses, cows, sheep, and goats grazed lazily in the fields. Grand estates were nestled within the vast acreage.

Little Bennie was completely oblivious to the landscape. He was occupied by a hand held computer game that his father had given him for Christmas. Whatever was on the screen was taking his full attention. The sudden quiet allowed Katie to take in the scenery around her.

Golden grape vines glowed richly in the soft morning light. Scattered leaves rustled by in the gentle breeze. They fell on the open fields like soft, butterfly wings. After driving several miles of windy roads, Steven reached the entrance to the winery. The grand building possessed beautiful old world charm. They parked near the front by a large, bronze fountain. Bacchus, the Roman god of wine, sat immersed within its cascading water. He wore a crown of grape leaves. He smiled devilishly at the bronze, drunken muses that danced and played around him.

Camellia and Steven gently kissed goodbye. Before her husband went back to the van, he turned back and looked at the women. "Alright ladies, try to stay out of trouble. You are starting to remind me of Lucy and Ethel," he said laughing softly.

"We will try our best," they teased.

After saying their goodbyes, the women decided to explore the grounds before heading inside. The air was rich with the aroma of chimney smoke and clean mountain air. It was a perfect fall day.

"This is absolute Heaven. You have no idea how much I need this right now. Lizzie has been driving me crazy. One moment she's happy, the next hour she's in tears. She's completely lost in her boy crazy phase. She spends most of her time on the phone talking with her special friend from church," Camellia sighed.

"Oh, I noticed the young altar server last week," Katie replied.

"Yes, that's the one. His name is Jason Murphy. They have known each other for years through our church. I think she thinks of him as her boyfriend. Steven will not have it. Of course, we both agree that she is too young for a boyfriend. It's really a difficult situation. If we come down too hard on her, I know she is going to rebel and see him behind our backs. I think it would be better to let her be friends with the young man under our supervision. If she is going to be interested in a boy, at least he is one from a nice family, and involved in our faith. She wants to invite Jason to her Quinceañera next week. Steven is completely against the idea. They've been arguing about it for days. But I'm really happy that you will be joining us. Lizzie is really excited that you are going to come."

"I am honored you'd invite. I wouldn't miss it for the world! I've never attended one," Katie responded.

"Her dress is getting altered on Monday. We have the church booked and that is all set up for the ceremony. We just need to finish getting the band for the party."

Katie looked out at the vineyards lost in thought.

"What are you thinking?" Camellia asked.

She paused before answering. "Do you believe in reincarnation?"

Her eyes were filled with curiosity.

"Well, that is a very interesting question. I have wondered about it before. Our faith teaches us that there is only one life gifted to us. As I understand it, you are going to one of three places when you die. Heaven, Hell, or Purgatory. There is no mention of coming back in another life in the Bible as far as I know. Truthfully, once is more than enough for me. Don't get me wrong. I love my life. It's just the thought of starting over and facing life's struggles again is very troubling to me. I don't like the thought of being separated from my family."

"I know." Katie hesitated for a moment and continued, "It's a troubling idea. Perhaps we'll get another chance if we've left unfinished business or if our life ended too soon. Maybe our love ones join us in the next life?"

"It's an overwhelming thought. I think this is it. Once we die, we join God in Heaven. What makes you bring up this interesting topic, my friend?"

She hesitated before answering. Katie wanted desperately to share everything that she was going through with Camellia. Yet, there were things that she even had a hard time believing. She considered describing some of the less dramatic events that had taken place.

"I've had some troubling dreams over the last several weeks. I've had vivid memories of living in Ireland during the 19th century. The Potato Famine was just beginning. I can remember my mother, my home in Kinvara, Galway, working on my farm. I recalled the love of my life. His name was Daniel McCarthy. The memories are very real to me," she sighed.

"That sounds really interesting. I want to hear more about the love of your life!" Camellia smiled brightly.

Katie returned the smile and shyly looked down at her small hands.

"I've also had some frightening moments in the cabin. I could hear what sounded like voices coming from the walls." She hesitated wanting to explain more. "I know this must sound pretty crazy. I wouldn't blame you if you wanted to call the people in white coats to take me away."

Camellia regarded her friend with kindness and understanding.

"Never be ashamed of your feelings or dreams, Katie. Women ignore their instincts. I'm sure the incident with that awful teddy bear was terribly frightening and traumatic. It would be surprising if you did not have any issues after that crazy discovery. You know, if you would like, we could get Father Peter to bless your house."

Katie's face brightened.

"That's a wonderful idea. I would love that. Let's give him a call this week. Would you mind joining us in the blessing, Camellia?"

"Absolutely, I was already planning on it," she smiled.

CHAPTER 24

With heavy issues weighing on both of their minds, they were more than happy to let off some steam at the winery. They eagerly made their way to the grand building and signed in for their private tour. A young woman quickly walked over. Her high heels clicked across the tile floors. Her delicate features were framed in a short, blond bob. She enthusiastically introduced herself as Jane Fitzgerald. Her tall, slender figure was set off nicely in a pair of tailored white slacks, high heels, and a pink cardigan. The scent of floral perfume engulfed her.

"Hello ladies! I will be your guide today," she flashed them a smile. "Your morning will begin with a private tour around the beautiful grounds of Bacchus Winery. You will experience the history of the chateau and valley, as well as the process of winemaking. We'll follow that with a private tasting of our best wines. And finally, you will enjoy a specially catered lunch, set in the middle of the vineyard, surrounded by the gorgeous Napa Valley Mountains. How does that sound?" The women smiled at their guide. "Oh and one more thing, I wanted to mention." She looked down briefly at her notebook. "Your gift package has recently been upgraded and we will be having a small surprise to start off this beautiful morning!"

"Ooh sounds exciting." Camellia answered. "I wonder what my hubby is up to, Katie?"

They laughed at the mysterious possibilities, and followed their tour guide outside to an open tour van. They climbed into a comfortable set of seats on top of the vehicle. They began their tour of the scenic grounds. The cool, morning air was refreshing against their skin as they toured the estate. Vibrant fall colors shimmered in the morning sun. It was another picturesque day in Napa Valley.

The vehicle followed the road, which led to a large, open clearing surrounded by several large oak trees. The women stepped down from their seats and climbed down the ladder, back to the lower level. They carefully made their way out of the bus and stood looking out at the large, wooden containers placed inside the circle of trees. They walked over to the tall barrels and looked over the rims. The large vats were packed with colorful grapes. A deep aroma of oak and juice was sharp and pleasantly rich. Their guide joined them and began a brief history of winemaking.

"The grape stomping tradition dates back as far as the early Roman Empire. The ancient process allows for the perfect release of juice from the skin of the grape, producing a delicious and flavorful wine. Ladies, you're going to experience firsthand what ancient civilizations practiced so many years ago!" she explained excitedly.

She clapped her hands and announced happily, "Your private tour has been recently upgraded to include the authentic grape stomping experience for yourselves!"

The women's eyes widened and they looked at each other. They tried their best not to laugh at their young guide's enthusiasm.

"Camellia, your husband was not kidding when he said that we are becoming like Lucy and Ethel!"

Without missing a beat, they slipped off their shoes and carefully placed them by the picnic table. There were several barrels in the field. Camellia and Katie looked at each other, smiled, and headed over to the largest barrel. Together, they held each other by the hand and carefully climbed inside the tall oak container. Tentatively, they stepped down into the gooey collection of wet grapes.

They burst out laughing as the cold grape juice filled the spaces in between their toes.

"Alright ladies, it's grape stomping time!"

Their guide's enthusiasm was contagious, and they soon found themselves eagerly smashing the chilly fruit. Jane happily walked over to the picnic table and turned on the large CD player. Within moments, Italian Opera music began to play forth from the speaker.

"Oh wow, they don't miss a thing," Camellia laughed.

The cold juice squished and splattered with their stomping motions. The bottom of the barrel was extremely slippery and wet. They stomped up and down while holding their skirts to their knees. Finding their balance was difficult. After a few minutes, the women found a nice rhythm.

The cold grape juice spattered over their legs and feet, leaving them feeling cold in the cool, autumn breeze.

"I think we might have a new hobby!" Camellia called out laughing. "Can you grow some grapes on your land?"

"Um, I think this is a one shot deal for me, Camellia." Katie called back.

She turned toward her friend, grinning, and suddenly slipped inside the barrel. She shrieked loudly as she lost her balance. Camellia grabbed her hands to steady her before she fell into the container. They laughed in unison. The grapes gradually turned to liquid.

After their adventure, their guide helped them climb out from the barrel. She offered them clean plastic containers, full of warm water, to wash off. They towel dried their legs and feet and put their heels back on.

"I took some great photos of you ladies. I will give you copies before you leave," Jane remarked.

"Steven is going to love this!" Camellia replied.

They went back to the tour bus and climbed the ladder to their seats. They drove around the grounds taking in the lush landscape surrounded by the autumn colored Napa Valley Hills.

Once the tour was over, they made their way back to a large building containing the chateau's enormous wine cellar. They entered into a darkened room with rows of oak barrels. The private entry room was inviting. Several vintage photographs depicting the winery in the twenties and thirties covered the walls. Afterwards, they were given a lengthy lesson on the region's prestigious awards and impressive history. Jane guided the women down a long hall, which led to a tasting room.

A grand table setting was waiting for them. The entire room, including the floors, walls, and furniture, was a rich polished walnut wood.

An enormous candle lit chandelier hung above the long, antique table. The lighting was soft, relaxing. The wall behind the table housed hundreds of bottles of fine wines. They were stacked to the ceiling. The women were offered a variety of wine samplings. Katie was impressed with several dry white and Chardonnay blends. Camellia seemed drawn to the rich Cabernet and Shiraz collection. They took their time sampling the various spirits. The guide was happy to answer questions and seemed thrilled by their enthusiasm.

This was followed by their personally assisted lunch overlooking the incredible Napa Valley Mountains. The ladies were more than satisfied from their delicious five course meal and wine pairings. Afterwards, they headed to The Bacchus Winery Gift Shop. They ended up purchasing several bottles of wine to take home. By the time Steven arrived to pick them up, they could barely keep their eyes open from all of the wine and food they had consumed. Steven smiled to himself as the girls slept peacefully on their drive home.

CHAPTER 25

Katie and Camellia were able to arrange a house blessing with Father Peter on Friday morning after the children were dropped off at school. Camellia arrived around ten. The ladies sat down in the breakfast nook together. Katie had decorated her table with her best place settings including her new Galway tea set. Little violets and roses adorned the fine china. A plate of lemon bars was neatly piled onto a large antique pastry server. She had picked up the fresh treats at the bakery on Main Street earlier that morning. They enjoyed their delicious Irish tea and fresh baked dessert as the morning sun streamed through the dining room window.

"Well, Katie, I hope you don't mind multi-tasking," she sighed. "Steve set up an appointment with his security alarm company at ten thirty. It looks like it's around the same time Father Peter will be performing the house blessing."

"That's not a problem, sweetie. I really appreciate the help. It will be a relief to have the security system and the blessing completed on the same day."

After saying this, a loud knock came from behind the door. Katie stood up and answered it. A heavy-set man stood patiently on the front porch. He smiled and introduced himself.

"Hi. I'm Daryl Johnson. Steve set up an appointment to have your alarm put in."

"Oh please come in. I'm Katie O'Brien." Camellia smiled brightly at Daryl. "Can I get you some coffee or tea before you start, Daryl?"

"Oh, that would be wonderful. A cup of coffee would really hit the spot. I just need to know where a couple of your outlets are and I can figure out the rest. I'll let you know when it's all ready. We will have it set up in no time," he smiled kindly.

"Thank you so much. It's a real relief."

Katie grabbed another mug from the cabinet to prepare his coffee. As she carried it over, a knocking began at the door.

"Thank you, Katie," he remarked as he took the cup.

She eagerly walked over to the door and was greeted warmly by Father Peter. The small man stood smiling on the porch.

"Hello, Katie. It's a pleasure to come visiting your lovely home this fair morning."

Katie led Father Peter gently by the arm and guided him to the breakfast nook.

"Hello Father! It's wonderful to see you," Camellia happily greeted him.

Daryl smiled and gave a quick hello. After introductions were made, Father Peter took a quick look around the room and smiled brightly.

"Well then, Katie, your home is filled with such lovely antiques!"

"Oh yes, several of the pieces were passed down to me from Ireland. They are treasures."

"Ah yes. To be true. Now, where would you like me to begin, Katie?"

"Well father, if you don't mind, I thought we might start in my bedroom."

"Wonderful," he answered.

Katie led Father Peter and Camellia to the back of the cabin. As the priest walked toward her room, his smile slowly faded. His entire demeanor had changed. His light-hearted expression suddenly switched to a serious, contemplative look.

"Father, is something wrong?" Katie asked.

He walked around the room and stopped at the end of her bed. Gradually, he looked up to the ceiling and his eyes locked on the thick varnish above. Outside, a cloud passed over the sun, and the room darkened. After a moment, he seemed to gather his thoughts and looked up seriously at the two women.

"Young lady, I don't mean to alarm you, but I have just a few questions to ask."

"Yes, of course, Father please ask me whatever you would like." Father Peter continued to speak.

"You mentioned that you were concerned about a recent trespassing incident that occurred in your yard. Have there been any other strange occurrences that have taken place since?"

She had given him a few details concerning the trespassing when she had made the appointment for the blessing. Katie took a deep breath before she answered. She knew that she had no choice but to speak the truth to the Father.

"Yes, there have been some other incidents, I'm afraid."

Camellia looked startled at the news.

"Actually, there have been unusual occurrences since the day that I moved in. I began having strange dreams the very first night that I slept in the cabin. Several of these dreams have taken place in Ireland. I recalled a detailed past life in the town of Kinvara near Galway Bay."

Father Peter interrupted. "I'm very familiar with that town, my dear. I've visited many times over the years."

"I have never been to Ireland. I have heard stories from my relatives. In my dreams, however, I can remember the faces of family members and friends that I have never met. In fact, they do not even belong to our time. My dreams depict Ireland during the nineteenth century."

She hesitated and quickly looked back and forth between Camellia and Father Peter. Their kind eyes silently encouraged her to go on with her story. She took a deep breath and continued.

"There is a man in my dreams named James Williams. He seems intent on hurting me. I have distinct memories where he did in fact take my life on the shores of Galway Bay."

Camellia gasped in astonishment as she continued.

"I remember details and events of *The Great Famine* in Ireland. I can see the old farm and my family's home. The blight eventually hit our land."

Father Peter quietly made the sign of the cross.

"Oh it was a terrible time, indeed, for the people of Ireland. There was great suffering all over the island to be sure."

"Yes, my mother used to tell me stories that had been passed down to her from my ancestors. Yet, these dreams are so much more than stories for me. I can remember, as if the memories were my own, as if I lived during that time. They seem so real."

"Have you had other experiences, child…in the home itself?"

"Yes, I'm afraid I have."

Camellia's eyes were full of wonderment and worry as Katie continued with her story.

"The other evening, when I was taking a bath, I heard some strange voices. They sounded like they were coming from the walls," she whispered quietly.

"And then…"

She hesitated, shifting her gaze between Father Peter and Camellia. She could not believe that she was saying this out loud. What would they think? Her voice began to choke up as she tried to find the words to describe the terrifying evening.

"The voices seemed to be coming from the cabin walls," she whispered. "They became loud and frantic, eventually overlapping one other. A powerful storm was brewing that particular evening. There was an unusual gust of wind outside and the lights suddenly went out altogether. The room became very cold. As my eyes tried to adjust to the dim light, a strange shadow appeared in the corner of the bathroom. At first the image seemed like that of a stranger. Eventually his features became more solid. I realized that it was James Williams. But then," she stopped for a moment to gather her thoughts, "the image began to change. It transformed into some kind of creature or monster, a demon. I've never seen anything so terrifying in my life."

Camellia's eyes grew wide and she quickly made the sign of the cross.

She stopped suddenly, somewhat in shock of what she had just heard herself say. Now she thought, now they knew that she had really lost her mind.

"What happened next, Katie?" Father Peter gently asked.

"It was as if my body had become parylzed. The creature moved toward me until it was standing over the tub. In an instant, a bright light appeared. An angel stood directly over the demon. I knew his face. His name is Daniel. I've seen him in my dreams of Ireland. I remembered him from my past life. He stood over the creature and commanded it to leave in the name of Jesus Christ. It fled when he lifted up a Pewter Cross and raised it toward him." Her words trailed off. Did she really just tell them all of her secrets?"

Father Peter looked deeply into Katie's tear filled eyes.

"There, there, my child. Do not be afraid. You are not losing your mind, my dear. Of course, this is definitely no commonplace occurrence by any means. When you have been a priest as long as I have, you come across God's mysteries time and again. It sounds as if your angel was sent by God to protect you. The Lord is merciful and his angels surround us with his light and love. I don't mean to frighten you, but I must be honest. You may be in great danger. We will need to find out the nature of this ungodly demon. There are great mysteries in the world that cannot be explained by science or philosophy. Gateways are sometimes opened to the spiritual realm. When a door opens to evil, we must do our best to close it."

His kind words were soothing. Her heart was filled with relief and gratitude, as he seemed to take the burden from her.

"Oh Father, thank you so much. I've been so afraid to talk about this."

Camellia quickly walked over to Katie and put her arm protectively over her shoulder.

"My poor friend, what a worry this must have been for you. This is what you were trying to tell me that day in the vineyard?"

"Yes. There is still so much I need to tell you. I am so lucky to have you in my life, Camellia."

"Katie, I love you like a sister. You are not alone in this."

"Indeed." Father Peter broke in. "Our Heavenly Father is always present watching over us. We are truly never alone. He is far more powerful than any evil in the world. Katie, I'm going to do a standard house blessing. This should keep you safe and protected. However, I want you to contact me immediately if you have any other occurrences. We will do whatever it takes to protect you, my dear. Further steps will be taken if needed."

"Father, do you mean an exorcism of the house?" Katie asked in a fearful tone.

"We will cross that bridge only, if, and when it is needed."

"Thank you, Father."

The priest opened his briefcase and carefully arranged his religious materials for the house blessing. He placed the silk vestment over his shoulders and quietly prayed.

"Restore unto me, O Lord, the stole of immortality, which was lost through the guilt of our first parents: and, although I am unworthy to approach. Your sacred Mysteries, nevertheless grant unto me eternal joy."

He took out a small glass jar of holy water. Carefully, he filled his silver aspergillum with the precious drops. With his Bible in hand, he began the ceremony of the house blessing. He began with the words, "In the name of the Father, the Son, and the Holy Spirit."

The women joined him as he made the sign of the cross. Father Peter, Katie, and Camellia responded, "Amen."

Father Peter continued the blessing by praying.

"When Christ took flesh though the Blessed Virgin Mary, he made his home with us. Let us now pray that he will enter this home and bless it with his presence. May he always be here among us; may he nurture our love for each other, share our joys, comfort us in our sorrows. Inspired by his teachings and example, let us seek to make our home before all else a dwelling place of love, diffusing far and wide the goodness of Christ. Peace be with this house and with all who live here. Blessed be the name of the lord."

Katie and Camellia responded, "Amen."

Father Peter then instructed Katie to read aloud from the Bible. She gently held it in her hands and read aloud in a strong voice.

"A reading from the letter of Paul to the Colossians

> You are God's chosen race, his saints; He loves you, and you should be clothed in sincere compassion, in kindness and humility, gentleness and patience.
>
> Bear with one another; forgive each other as soon as a quarrel begins. The Lord has given you; now you must do the same.
>
> Over all these clothes, to keep them together and complete them, put on love.
>
> And may the peace of Christ reign in your hearts, because it is for this that you were called together as parts of one body. Always be thankful.
>
> Let the message of Christ, in all its richness, find a home with you. Teach each other, and advise each other, in all wisdom. With gratitude in your hearts sing psalms and hymns and inspired songs by God; And never say or do anything except in the name of the Lord Jesus, giving thanks to God the Father through him."

In a powerful voice she finished with, "The word of the Lord."

Father Peter and Camellia responded, "Thanks be to God."

The gentle priest took a moment, and then looked up to the ceiling. He paused for a brief moment as he gathered his thoughts. He began to pray.

"Protect us, Lord, as we awake; watch over us as we sleep, that awake we may keep watch with Christ, and asleep, we may rest in peace.

Grant this through Christ our Lord. Amen."

The women followed Father Peter into the bathroom, where they gathered around the claw- foot tub. Katie tried her best to not think of the demonic creature that had appeared before her in this room. Father Peter read aloud in a strong voice.

"Blessed are you, Lord of heaven and earth. You formed us in wisdom and love. Refresh us in body and spirit, and keep us in good health that we might serve you.

Grant this through Christ our Lord. Amen."

He spent extra time in the two rooms with the most recent activity. He sprinkled holy water as he moved through them. As he entered down the hallway leading into the kitchen, the alarm specialist's eyes widened as Father Peter read aloud from the Bible. The women echoed back various verses. Finally, the priest stood in the doorway facing the cabin with outstretched arms.

"God bless this house," he said in a loud and authoritative voice. He lifted the silver aspergillum high in the air. He shook it firmly as a long spray of holy water shot out of the silver encasing.

They finished the blessing together by saying, "Amen." And made the sign of the cross.

"Katie, I have one more ceremony to perform before I leave."

The women followed him back to the bedroom where the blessing had commenced. Father Peter took out an emerald green rosary from the pocket of his briefcase. He offered it to both Katie and Camellia. They gently kissed it. He placed it on the nightstand and said, "I hope this will give you comfort, Katie. You can say the Rosary whenever you want to draw closer to Jesus and the Virgin Mary."

"Oh Father, thank you so much for your kindness and understanding. I can't thank you enough for all that you have done for me today," she said with tears welling in her eyes.

"Oh my child, you are very welcome. I want you to get in touch is you need anything else."

"I will, Father."

After the ceremony was completed, the women walked Father Peter outside to his car. Cozy the Goose ran over as he bobbed his head from side to side. The priest smiled brightly at the bird. "Well, what a fine looking goose. What a site for sore eyes. We have plenty of geese back in Ireland. They are good protectors to be sure. Looks like you have one more guardian on your side, Katie."

He smiled at them as he made his way back to his car. After he drove away, the women walked back to the cabin. The technician was just finishing installing the security box near the front door. He showed Katie how to plug in the code and how to deactivate it if it went off.

"If you have a break in, and the alarm is not turned off in the five minutes time window, 911 will be called and emergency vehicles will be sent to your home. With your new security system and your house blessing, you're in good hands," Daryl smiled.

"Thank you so much. It's wonderful."

Katie signed all of the paperwork. He gave her a pamphlet detailing all of the systems codes and instructions. The women said goodbye and he headed out to his car.

When they were alone, Camellia asked Katie if they could sit out on the porch swing for a moment. The women sat down and looked out onto the forested yard. The ravens cawed loudly in the distance.

"I'm sure this is more than you bargained for when we became friends," Katie trailed off. She looked intently out at the view as hot tears stung her eyes.

Camellia looked calmly at her friend, and then took her hands gently. "Katie, I'm about to tell you something that I've only shared with a handful of my closest family members."

The women looked intently at one another.

"In my family, on my mother's side, the women have what you might call a special sense. The gift, or as my family calls it, Las Dotes, has been passed down to me by my mother and so on. I have always had a special way of telling when a person possesses good or bad energy, if they are truthful or not. There have been events in my life that I knew would happen. I knew the moment we met that we were going to be wonderful friends," she smiled.

She lifted Katie's hand and patted the back of it.

"You glow with kindness and honesty. I could see it right from the start. In some people, you can almost see a kind of life force, or, an aura some call it. Your aura glows a beautiful blue around your body."

Katie eyes widened in amazement.

"Can you describe what this looks like to you, Camellia?"

She was quiet for a moment as she tried to find the right words.

"It's kind of like looking at rain puddles on the ground after a stormy day. Sometimes, the light hits the water in a way that sends prisms that reflect the sunlight. Your blue aura looks like translucent light rippled on crystal water. Its vibrancy represents your kindness, compassion, and nurturing spirit. It's not an accident that you find yourself drawn to nature. And children. You are a nurturer. I could see the connection with my children the moment that we met. They absolutely adore you, and my husband is thrilled that I've found such a wonderful and caring friend.

I was aware of my gift on my twelfth birthday. I went to bed that night and had a vivid dream about my grandmother. I opened my eyes and could see her standing over my bed smiling lovingly down. She said it was her time to be with the angels and that my mother would need me since she was leaving. My grandmother kissed me on the forehead. She took my hand and said that she would always be close by. *Take care of your momma, little Cammy.*

In the morning, I woke up to my mother crying at the dining room table. My father was standing behind her with his hand on her shoulder trying to comfort her.

My father said softly, 'Cammy, I have some very sad news. Your abuela passed away last night.'

'I know daddy, she came to me last night and told me she was going to heaven.' I answered.

"I told my mother that my grandmother was with the angels now and not to be sad. She hugged me, knowing that my grandmother was at peace.

My dreams and feelings have always been something I've kept very private. Now, I see that the gift has been passed down to little Bennie. He's the first son in my family in generations to have it. Steven just sees his sensitivity as being a great way find the outcomes of football games," she laughed softly. "But I recognize the signs. He already has the ability to see right into the hearts of people. It's just a way of knowing. I think we're all capable of doing this on some level. The gift is just stronger for some.

I knew you were speaking the truth when you told us about your dreams and the frightening vision you had in your cabin. I'm just sorry you've been going through this alone. I sensed there were things you were not ready to share. I didn't want to overwhelm you with my insight. You see, you're not the only one that is afraid of being thought of as crazy," Camellia smiled.

"I'm here for you, Katie. I want you to tell me the minute anything unusual happens."

"Thank you so much. I can't tell you what this means to me," she answered happily.

"There's just one more thing. I don't want to frighten you, but I have the feeling that it's not over yet. I sense unfinished business. Just be alert right now. I wish that I could give you more information. It's just a feeling that I have."

"Thank you. I'll be very careful, and I will let you know if anything happens."

The women stood up and hugged each other tightly.

"I guess I better get going with the final preparations for the Quinceañera. Call me if you need anything!"

"I will."

After saying their goodbyes, Katie walked back inside the cabin and made her way to the kitchen table and sighed deeply. It had been a relief to confide in Father Peter and Camellia. Her gratitude for their support and kindness was humbling. She finished her tea and made her way outside to start another day of planting. She worked for hours at her potting bench. The remainder of the day eased her mind and her body. She slept peacefully that night. The rest of the week took on an ordinary schedule of errands, planting, and jogging breaks. She made time to visit one of the local boutiques to pick out her outfit for Quinceañera that Saturday. Katie chose a dark green satin dress for the special occasion. Everything seemed to be falling into place. Life's sharp edges were smoothed back into normalcy.

CHAPTER 26

The afternoon of Lizzie's Quinceañera was beautiful. Katie changed into her emerald green gown in the early afternoon. The color brought out the sparkling highlights in her bright eyes. She arrived at Saint Brigid's Cathedral at 2:30pm. The Sanchez family was waiting outside the church gathered around Father Peter discussing last minute details for Mass.

Steven happily introduced his parents, Rosa and Carl Sanchez. They warmly embraced and welcomed her to Mass. Camellia was excited for her father to meet Katie. Robert Juarez was a tall man in his early seventies, with a kind face and quiet demeanor. He smiled happily as he chatted about the upcoming ceremony. He offered his arm and escorted her to the front pew.

Soon the church was filled with friends and family members eagerly anticipating the Thanksgiving Mass. Once all of the family members were seated, the church choir began to play the opening hymn, as the procession made its way down the aisle. Jason Murphy led the group proudly carrying the procession cross. Lizzie elegantly followed behind. She wore a satin purple ball gown. Layers of rich chiffon fabric rolled gracefully down to the floor. Her delicate waist cinched within the cascading layers. She held a bouquet of lavender roses. The flowers matched the rosy glow of her cheeks. Her parents escorted her on each side, followed by ten of her closest friends in boy/girl pairs. Father Peter was last in line.

Camellia looked absolutely stunning next to her beautiful daughter. She wore a rose color satin gown, which complimented her dark eyes. The Mass was dedicated to Lizzie. After Father Peter's Homily, Lizzie's God Parents were instructed to come forward. Her God Mother presented her with a silver pendant with an image of the Virgin of Guadalupe, The Patron Saint of Mexico. Her God Father gifting her with a silver tiara followed this. He placed it gently on her head and kissed her on the cheek.

Lizzie smiled and thanked them for the beautiful gifts. Afterwards, she placed her bouquet of lavender roses on the church altar in honor of The Virgin Mary. After Mass, the entire family took turns thanking Father Peter and headed over to downtown Napa to celebrate Lizzie's Quinceañera.

They arrived at the large banquet hall around 5:30. There were several tables decorated with white satin table covers, fine porcelain settings, and crystal goblets. Each table had a large, floral arrangement containing lavender roses. The fresh aroma of fresh Mexican cuisine filled the room. Once everyone was seated, Camellia's parents escorted their daughter to the front of the hall. Steven took the mike and began to speak once the audience finally quieted.

"My little girl has truly blossomed into a beautiful young lady." The crowd clapped loudly as he spoke. He gently placed his hand on her shoulder.

"Lizzie stole my heart the minute she was born. As you ready yourself to enter the world of adulthood, I present you with this doll, to remind you of the childhood you're leaving behind. As you turn the page of this new chapter in your life remember that your family, and that the Lord Jesus Christ walks beside you in your journey."

Steven choked on these last words. He leaned down and kissed her on the cheek. Lizzie gently took the little doll from her father. The bright purple on the doll matched her dress.

"Thank you, daddy. I love you so much!" She reached up and kissed him on the cheek.

The room filled with applause as family members and friends clapped and cheered.

Then, Steven's mother approached the stage. She smiled and presented her granddaughter with a pair of dark purple high heel shoes. Carefully placing them on her feet, she said, you will wear these new shoes as you step into womanhood. This gift should remind you that you are not alone in your new journey. You belong to a sisterhood that embraces you now and forever." She kissed her on the cheek.

"Thank you, abuela." Lizzie hugged her tightly.

Camellia's eyes filled with tears as she watched the scene unfold. She turned to Katie and whispered, "*The Changing of the Shoes* dates back to the Mayan civilization. It represents Lizzie entering the world of womanhood, while Steven's gift of *The Last Doll* symbolizes the end of her girlhood." Katie nodded as she learned the various meaning of the symbolic and religious ceremonies. After the *Changing of the Shoes* ceremony was completed, the band played a formal waltz. Steven took his daughter's hand and asked, "May I have this dance?"

She smiled happily and took his arm. Steven beamed and escorted her to the dance floor. Tears ran down Camellia's face as she watched them dance. Whatever arguments the two had been having was resolved. Lizzie smiled lovingly up at her father as the song slowly came to the end. Now it was time for her date to join her on the dance floor. Jason Murphy came forward from the crowd wearing a handsome gray suit adorned with a purple silk tie. He walked up to Steven and politely asked his permission to dance with his daughter. Katie noticed Camellia holding her breath as she watched. Steven looked at him for a moment and said, "Take good care of her, son."

"I most definitely will. Thank you, sir."

With that, the young man escorted Lizzie to the middle of the dance floor. The couple smiled shyly at one other, making occasional eye contact as they twirled around the room. Eventually, the family members joined in until everyone was dancing and enjoying the music.

Steven walked back and sat next to his wife. His eyes glistened. Camellia took his hand in hers and leaned on his shoulder.

After the song ended, Camellia's father stood up and politely asked if Katie would join him in a dance. She happily accepted his invitation. He gently took her by the arm and led her to the dance floor. He swept her off her feet with his graceful dance moves. Camellia and Steven joined them soon after. Some time later, their dancing had made them very hungry, and they headed over to the banquet for their meal.

Camellia had made sure to have an assortment of vegetarian options available for her friend. Katie enjoyed the corn and cheese tamales with a glass of cold sangria. She had put away two tamales and was working of a third, when she noticed Bennie slowly drifting off to sleep in his mother's arms. Camellia ran her fingers through his hair as he snored softly in her arms. It had been a long day for him.

The ballroom music eventually turned to livelier pop and hip-hop songs. Lizzie and her friends were soon rocking out with all of their latest dance moves. The adults sat back and watched. Time flows forever onward as the younger generations take their place in the dance of life.

CHAPTER 27

Katie woke on Halloween morning feeling fresh and renewed. The Quinceañera had been moving. She smiled to herself thinking about the special day. She soon set about her routine of a morning jog, a shower and change of clothes followed by a day of planting. Cozy The Goose followed her eagerly around the yard. She gave him a large bowl of salad greens and water and set them by her potting bench. She enjoyed his company while she worked. Dark clouds gradually moved in around noon. Katie worried that Camellia's children would be dealing with a storm during their Halloween adventures. She stopped work at about four and went back to the cabin. It took some time to wash the dirt from her hands and underneath her fingernails. Planting could be messy at times. She went back to her wardrobe and chose a black long sleeve cotton shirt with a fuzzy ghost on the front. The word *Boo* was written in large letters underneath. She slipped on a pair of black jeans and matching boots. Her hair flowed down her shoulders. As the sun was setting, Katie heard the Sanchez van pull into the driveway. The whole family was present along with one additional guest. In the back next to Lizzie, sat Jason Murphy. Steven was behind the wheel. His usual relaxed demeanor had been replace by a serious scowl. Camellia sat in the front seat and made eye contact with her friend. Her expression conveyed that it might be a long night.

The children were all beaming with excitement, anticipating the evening's adventure. They had chosen characters from one of the popular teen vampire series that the sisters were currently reading. Camellia had helped design the costumes. She had spent quite a bit of time altering and fitting the dresses. They looked ready to step on a movie set.

Bennie's hair was slicked back and gelled. He wore a black silk vest and trousers covered over in a red, silk cape. Lizzie and Jessie wore long dresses, black wigs, and pale makeup. The older sister's bright, hazel eyes stood out dramatically with her smoky eyeliner and mascara. A red, velvet dress flowed down to her ankles. Black ankle boots completed her gothic outfit. Katie wondered how she managed to leave the house with her protective dad at home. Jason wore a stylish red vest under a smoking jacket and dark pleated trousers.

"Where are all of the children, Camellia? All I see are a bunch of beautiful vampires."

The children giggled and Katie played along. The family drove down to a well-lit neighborhood. Camellia locked arms with Katie as they walked. The children rushed ahead to trick-or-treat at the lavish homes.

"How are you doing, my friend? Is all well at the O'Brien cabin?"

"Yes, thank you for asking. It was such a relief to have the security system put in. The house blessing really gave me such peace of mind. I have been sleeping like a baby all week," she smiled.

"Wonderful. You've been in our thoughts and prayers."

Thank you so much for inviting me trick-or-treating. This is so fun. Halloween has always been one of my favorite holidays."

"Mine too. It's the best!"

The adults waited patiently as the children went door to door. Their bags were growing by the moment. Bennie ran back to Camellia and Katie and announced, "The nice lady gave me two candy bars instead of one!"

"That's wonderful," the women answered.

"Would you like one, Katie?" His face became quite serious.

"Oh no thank you, sweetie. Save that for yourself. You're working hard tonight for all of your treats," she smiled.

"Thank you. I have plenty of candy if you need any," he assured her.

Katie smiled.

"Lizzie and her friend had been invited to a house party tonight. We didn't like the sound of it. We compromised by inviting Jason to join us for trick-or-treating. Teenagers are a tricky bunch. If I can just get Steven to stop glaring at him all night, I will be a happy woman," she laughed.

As they made their way down a block of decorated homes, the light began to set in the West. Dark scarlet streaks glowed in the muted light. Although the colors were beautiful, they left Katie with a feeling of unease and restlessness. Dark clouds eventually covered the entire night sky. The wind howled in the trees overhead.

"Looks like we might be ending our trick-or-treating early tonight. Feels like a storm is coming," Camellia remarked.

"It definitely does. Poor kiddos," Katie answered.

"Well, I have refreshments at the house. I also have several bottles of wine left over form our winery adventure," Camellia smiled.

"Wonderful. That means we don't have to stomp grapes tonight," Katie laughed.

The children were able to make it another block before the rain began to fall. They headed back to the van, and Jessie asked her parents permission to invite a couple of her girlfriends over to the house. She called them up while they drove home. The group reached the home just as the storm let loose. Everyone headed into the kitchen. As usual, Camellia was fully prepared. She had a batch of Halloween cookies, brownies, chips, and popcorn. Several pumpkins and gourds rested on the marble counter top. Camellia turned on the CD players. Spooky Halloween music and ghostly moans set the mood. The children picked out their favorite pumpkins and carried them over to the dining room table. Bennie had chosen a nice, large one. Steven gave his son an approving smile.

"Son, that looks like a winner!"

The table was covered with a Halloween tablecloth. There were pumpkin carving tools, stencils, paints, glitter, and sequins on top. The children took their seats and began to work on their creations. Steven helped his son cut out the top of his pumpkin. He showed him how to carve at an angle so the top would lock into place. Bennie giggled as his sisters helped him shovel out the insides of the pumpkin.

"Ok, place all of the pumpkin fillings over here." Camellia set down a large ceramic bowl on the table. "I need a volunteer to sort out the seeds for baking," she explained.

Lizzie happily volunteered. Jason helped her with the messy job. They carefully removed the seeds from the soggy pumpkin meat. Every once in awhile they would make eye contact and smiled shyly at one another. Steven proudly worked alongside Bennie. They had chosen a pickup truck stencil. Together, they traced the truck pattern on the large gourd.

Katie helped Camellia bring back the bowls of pumpkin seeds to the kitchen. As she rinsed the seeds, Camellia went to the fridge and retrieved a cold bottle of Napa Valley Chardonnay. She poured them each a generous glass.

"Thank you. This is absolutely perfect."

Katie washed her hands and dried them on the towel by the sink. The ladies toasted one another. As their glasses, clanked, a large streak of lightening lit up the kitchen window. They both laughed as they jumped from the sound of the loud strike. The children shrieked with excitement from the dining room.

"Wow," Steven remarked, "That definitely sets the mood for a spooky Halloween night."

"Oh sweetie, I picked up some of your favorite autumn beer from the store today." Camellia replied.

"Thank you, my love."

He opened the fridge and took out a bottle. Camellia retrieved an old-fashioned beer stein from the cabinet and set it down for her husband. Bubbles rose to the surface of the glass as he poured the beer.

"I better get back to the children, dear." He gave his wife a quick peck on the cheek and went back to the table to join the young people.

"I don't think he's going to leave Lizzie alone with Jason for one minute tonight. Gives a whole new meaning to over-protective father!" They both laughed as Camellia busied herself making cocoa.

She handed Katie a Halloween apron and took one for herself. Katie's apron sported a big black cat in front of a harvest moon. Camellia's apron was black with little pumpkins. A witch flew over the field.

"You are truly amazing. I absolutely love all of your Halloween decorations and treats."

"Thank you, Katie. I'm so excited to finally find a friend that loves Halloween as much as I do. I still can't believe how beautiful your antique Halloween collection is. It's truly breathtaking."

"Thank you. I've been collecting them for years. A few were passed down from my great-grandparents. There's nothing creepier than some of those old Irish Halloween decorations. Did you know that the original jack-o'-lanterns were made from turnips?"

"Really? That is interesting."

"Yes, they're pretty scary looking. I can't imagine trying to carve a turnip," she laughed.

The ladies chatted about some of their favorite Halloween adventures over the years. Soon the room was filled with the scent of hot chocolate and cinnamon. After warming up the chocolate and milk, Camellia poured the cocoa into mugs and topped them off with a generous portion of orange and white marshmallows. She carried the serving tray decorated with Halloween themed mugs into the dining room. The children excitedly took their cups and continued working on their pumpkin masterpieces. The spooky music continued to pour out moaning, chains, rattling, and cackling witches in the background. The evening was perfect- the weather, the company, the food and drink. As the night came to a close, the children brought out their jack-o'-lanterns to the front porch. Steven placed a tea light inside each one.

"Looks like we have some amazing artists," Katie remarked.

Steven and Bennie had created an impressive dump truck carving on their large pumpkin. Jessie and her girlfriends, Amanda and Cynthia, had used their horse and unicorn stencils. Finally, Lizzie and Jason placed their jack-o'-lantern next to the others. The large heart-shaped etching glowed brightly in the candlelight. They took turns admiring one other's creations.

"Well children, it's getting pretty late." Camellia said with a yawn. "It's a school night."

Bennie ran over to Katie and gave her a big hug.

"Goodnight, sweetie," she said hugging him back.

Steven volunteered to drive Katie and the children's friends home. They tiredly said their goodbyes and called it a night.

CHAPTER 28

Katie was exhausted by the time she arrived back to the cabin. She thanked Steven for the ride and headed inside. His last stop would be to drop off Jason at his house. She wondered what Steven would say to the young man once she left the van. Poor kid. She smiled at the thought. The alarm started to beep as she unlocked the door. She hurried over to the security panel, and keyed in the code to deactivate the alarm. She went into the bathroom and washed her face and changed into pajamas.

She drifted to sleep as the soft rain caressed the beams of the old log cabin. Moments later, Katie found herself inside a child's bedroom. Big yellow tractors and oversized truck posters covered the walls. She realized that she was standing in Bennie's room. She was not sure how or why she was there. Straining her eyes in the darkness, she began making her way across the floor. Moonbeams illuminated a small boy sitting by himself in the dark. He appeared unusually transfixed by an object that he was holding in his hands. His right hand moved in a circular motion. Strange, garbled metallic sounds grinded out of the object in an eerily pitched melody. She drew closer until she was standing directly behind him. She lowered herself down and spoke, "Bennie," she whispered. "What are you doing? Why aren't you in bed, sweetie?" her voice shook.

The child continued to focus on the strange toy. Each rotation of the handle sounded more urgent than the last, the old, metal sound of *Pop Goes the Weasel* played out slowly. The notes were high pitched and out of tune. The soft light of the moon drifted directly on them. She could now see the metal box clearly in the light.

Rusted paint appeared worn and cracked on the old antique. Underneath the chipped, peeling surface was an image of a log cabin in the woods. A tall, dark figure stood outside the window in the back of the home. Without warning, it began to move. Long outstretched arms reached toward the window. It continued to strike at the glass with its long claws. Katie could not tear her eyes away. The creature slowly turned its face until it looked directly at her. Its mouth turned up in a leering grin. Sharp, needle-like teeth emerged inside its gaping mouth. It moved and twisted along with the notes of the strange sounding music. As she strained to listen, she could hear the creature singing:

"Every night when I get home

The monkey's on the table, Take a stick and knock it off,

Pop! Goes the weasel."

Dark rust poured forth from the demon's eyes and ran down the side of the box. Bennie stopped cranking the handle of the strange toy. The metallic music came to an abrupt stop. He turned to face her, gripping the old antique in his hand. Without warning, a sharp popping burst from the tin box. The lid sprang open along with a terrifying growl. A moldy teddy bear emerged from the container. Its one remaining eye glowed crimson red. Its stitched smile pulled apart with a tearing sound revealing a full set of razor sharp fangs. Once freed, its mouth began to open and close. Gore and decay spilled forth from its gaping jaws. The putrid aroma filled the room. Maggots began to emerge and crawl loose from the bear's moth-eaten fur. Their swollen bodies fell onto the floor in pulsing heaps. Suddenly the boy awakened from his trance. He took Katie by the hand and screamed, "Run, Katie, Run!"

She immediately took the boy in her arms and ran for the bedroom door. The moment they reached the entrance, the room became dim and out of focus. They found themselves surrounded within a dense and heavy fog. To her horror, she felt Bennie's arms begin to slip from her neck. The child's small form slowly vanished into the mist. The room went pitch black and she heard the child's voice in the distance.

"Get out of your house, Katie! The monster is coming. Run!!!!!"

CHAPTER 29

Katie suddenly found herself sitting on the end of her bed disoriented and bewildered. The sound of loud, piercing beeping filled the interior of the house. It was joined with the storm raging outside her cabin. The wind and rain pounded violently against the wall of her bedroom. She realized that her security system alarm had been set off. She groggily left her bed, her head still reeling from her nightmare, to find out why the alarm had been triggered. An icy gust of wind blasted the side of her face as she stood up. She turned to her right and realized that the large bedroom window had shattered. Glass shards glowed in the bright moonlight. Her heart pounded in her chest as she frantically tried to find the light switch. She reached up as her hand touched the wall; a hot burning sensation grazed her skin. She screamed out in terror and pain. Turning abruptly around, she came face to face with James Williams.

He looked down at her with delight at her shock and confusion. The eyes shining in the moonlight were dark and soulless.

"Don't put on the light, my love. It will spoil the mood," he laughed deeply.

The nauseating scent of decay and old stale whiskey permeated the room.

"After all, this is our wedding night." He grabbed her painfully by both of her arms and pulled her tightly against his chest.

The proximity of his body was both intimate and horrifying. His touch sent tremors of revulsion and terror. She struggled in vain to release herself from his cruel embrace. The aroma of whiskey was heavy as his grip tightened and he pulled her closer. Underneath the aroma was the unpleasant odor of sulfur. The moonlight faded from the room and she was suddenly falling through time and space. She closed her eyes and prayed Daniel would find her.

CHAPTER 30

Daniel stood guard outside Katie's bedroom window. An eerie calm fell over the woods. The memory of his wedding day surfaced in his mind. Today would have been their anniversary. He watched the forest in silence. The harvest moon appeared like a swollen heart in the night sky. The wind whipped the trees and shook the branches overhead. Rain began to fall. As the storm gathered energy, another noise surfaced. He followed the sound until he reached a large oak tree. Standing in the moonlight was an old woman. She was dressed in black lace. Soft, muffled cries could be heard under her shimmering veil. Her wailing became louder and more urgent. The terrible sound seemed to emanate from her very soul. Daniel walked to her side and gently put a hand on the old woman's shoulder.

"What ails you, woman," he asked. As he withdrew his hand, the veil fell open to reveal a nightmare. Empty, black sockets. A gaping hole where her mouth should have been, a terrible keening erupting from the dark opening. The force of the cries shook the trees. And then there was silence.

The sound of shattering glass followed. Daniel hurried back to the cabin. The curtains from Katie's bedroom blew through the shattered window. He rushed into her bedroom, sword in hand, only to find it empty.

By the time Daniel realized Katie was missing, it was too late. The piercing sound of her alarm system raged inside.

The stench of whiskey was heavy in the air.

"No, this can't be," he announced angrily to the empty room. "Katie! Where are you?"

A rush of hot, damp air blew against his face. Pieces of plaster and varnish fell from the blistered ceiling. He closed his eyes as the reality sank in. His greatest fear had come true. Without hesitation, he flew upward, entering the portal. The empty void embraced him. Out of the darkness, a pin of light appeared. It grew larger as he drew closer. Dense fog surrounded him. He was standing on a cliff. Below, an endless trail of people marched along the spiraling path. Their cries carried on the wind. Daniel flew down to the ground, landing on the dry, desert floor.

A haggard looking man cried out in anguish, "I didn't mean it. I never meant to hurt her. It was an accident. Just an accident."

An elderly man grabbed Daniel's arm. He looked on pleadingly; his eyes overcome with despair.

"Have you seen my wife, sir? I can't seem to find her. Do you know where we are?" he asked.

Before Daniel could answer, the old man had disappeared back into the mist. A teenage girl stood in his place.

"Where is my baby brother? I left him alone just for a minute. Where did he go?" she asked in bewilderment.

Daniel's heart filled with pity for the lost souls. His wings outstretched before him and he flew back up into the oppressive sky. Looking on, he watched the endless procession descend further into the abyss. He searched for Katie on the trail. There was no sign of her anywhere.

The sound of thunder erupted above. Hot droplets fell on his skin. The colorful prisms glowed like Christmas lights. They changed to deep scarlet red blinding him with their intensity. Losing his balance, he fell towards the earth. Through space and time, he journeyed for what seemed like an eternity. And then, in an instant, he landed abruptly onto a cold, stone floor. He slowly stood up, straining his eyes in the darkness. He groped blindly, his arms outstretched. Muffled voices whispered behind him. In his confusion, he called out for his beloved:

"Katie, where are you?"

And then… a faint answer, "Daniel, I'm inside Dunguaire Castle. I'm trying to find my way to the West Wing. But, I'm lost."

But the voice faded way and he found himself once again embraced by dark silence.

CHAPTER 31

When she finally opened her eyes, the alarm had stopped; she was no longer in her bedroom. James moved away from her and walked across the room. Her eyes strained to adjust to the candlelight and darkness. Slowly, she looked around and realized she was standing in a great ballroom. A grand, antique fireplace burned earnestly against the back wall. The aroma was not unpleasant. Two Irish Coat of Arms were placed on each side of the fireplace. Above the mantel was an enormous ornate tapestry of a vividly white unicorn standing in a meadow. There was something familiar about the scene. Several large window alcoves were set deeply in the stone of the old room. The colorful glass took the brunt of the night's storm. Sheets of rain lashed across the delicately painted images of violets, clover, and roses. She fought a heavy fatigue and confusion trying desperately to make sense of the bizarre situation, despite her overwhelming sense of panic.

Outside the winds and rains roared --a roll of thunder echoed off in the distance. Bright light exploded within the room. Her eyes slowly adjusted. Pewter candleholders were placed throughout the space. Dramatic, ornate sconces lit up the walls. She walked toward the center of the room. A grand table was covered in white lace. There were two elegant table settings on each end of the long table. Several silver platters of various meats including fowl, venison, and pork filled the space. In the middle of the grand banquet was a silver antique plate. On top was a body of a large boar, head and all. A dark red apple rested inside its grinning mouth. The animal appeared to have been cooked over a spit. The rich aroma smelled pungent. She was not sure what was more horrifying, that there was a spread of dead animals on the table, or the fact that she had been kidnapped from her bedroom in the middle of the night. The thought was so absurd it nearly made her laugh aloud. But she stifled the urge. Out of the darkness, James appeared holding a large bouquet of pink roses. His boots echoed loudly on the stone floors. When he reached Katie, he bowed and held them up to her.

"For my lady."

Her mind raced as she tried to make sense of it all. On the one hand, her captor appeared in human form, which was better than the horrific manifestation from their last meeting. If his demonic appearance showed itself again, she feared that her mind would snap from the insanity of it all. Her survival instincts had been triggered the moment he made himself known in her bedroom. Perhaps she might appease him and keep him from losing his temper. Everything in her wanted just the opposite. She desperately yearned to scream in his face and attack him, though that would only get her so far. She took a deep breath and tried to stifle the anger.

"Thank you, James. They are beautiful," she quietly remarked. She took a small curtsy and looked down to the ground.

Her meekness in attitude seemed to work its magic. James smiled brightly and clapped his hands together like a small boy.

"Well, Ms. Katie, you finally remembered to call me James. Isn't that marvelous. This is much more pleasant than our last meeting. I'm afraid we got off on the wrong foot," he laughed loudly as he seemed to recall the memory. "But then again, young lovers are bound to get into little arguments now and again. Am I right, dear?"

She stared at him in complete disbelief. It was beyond comprehension that he could trivialize the violence and pain he had inflicted on her past life.

"It's been a long time since Ireland, my love. What do you think? Is it everything you imagined?"

As he said this, Katie's shock began to loosen its grip and she realized that they were inside Dunguaire Castle. This was the grand ballroom where her wedding reception was to have taken place many years ago. She had visited the castle with her parents as a child. Lady McClain had always been a kind and benevolent hostess during their visits.

She looked up and took in more details. Old antique ribbons, crepe paper, and white satin bows were decorated throughout the room. The decorations glowed and sparkled in the candlelight.

"We can finally have our wedding reception like we planned so many years ago," he grinned gleefully.

Startled, she looked up at his face. His dark eyes were a mixture of excitement, pain, and absolute insanity.

"Do you like it, my dear?"

Katie regained her composure and replied, "Oh yes, it's very beautiful, James. I like it very much."

The words felt obscene on her tongue. Self-preservation and instinct was moving her along.

"Oh, silly me," he laughed. "I almost forgot. Here, have a seat, my dear."

He walked over to the table and pulled out the old antique chair. Katie gingerly sat down on the velvet cushion.

"I have a special surprise for you."

He moved to the opposite end of the table. He returned holding a large box wrapped in white satin bows, and placed it carefully on her lap. "Open it, my love."

His eyes were wide with excitement and anticipation. She looked up and forced herself to smile at him. It was actually painful.

"Oh, James, you shouldn't have."

With shaking hands, she unwrapped the ribbons and slid the container open. An ivory wedding dress was folded neatly inside. She carefully pulled out the dress. Tears rose in her eyes as she realized that it was the wedding dress her mother had made her.

"I had it cleaned for you. I'm afraid it was, well, a little dirty from our silly quarrel that day."

He reached down and grabbed her right hand and kneeled on the floor. He looked up earnestly.

"You will be relieved to know, Katie, that I forgive you."

Her eyes widened as he spoke.

"You forgive me?" She asked in complete astonishment.

"Yes, I have had many years to think it over. Believe me, the years have mellowed me," he said, once again laughing in his high-pitched tone. "I realize that you were just playing hard to get. I'm afraid that I lost my temper with you. It's silly really," he laughed.

James explained the event as if taking the life of Daniel and her were trivial, bygones. She realized that his grip on reality had been lost long ago.

"I want you to put the dress on, Katie. I have the dressing area all set up for you." He pointed to the back of the room.

A curtained changing room was waiting. She could feel the blood draining from her face as she realized what he was planning.

"Oh now, don't you worry. I won't peek," he winked at her.

His flirting sent chills down her spine.

"There will be time for that later, on our wedding night." His grin widened, as he appeared to be imagining it. Her stomach cramped in repulsion at the thought.

"But first you must have some of the wonderful feast I had prepared just for you."

He picked up two razor sharp knives and began to sharpen them against each other. A flash of blue light sparked between the blades. The sound echoed within the walls of the castle. Slowly, he cut into the animal's flank. To her horror, blood began to pour forth in a syrupy river, which pooled around the serving tray. He slid the chunk of flesh onto a polished ceramic dinner plate. He carefully set the dish down in front of her on the table. He smiled happily as he served her. The odor of the poor, deceased animal made her stomach roll.

"I'm so sorry, James. I'm a vegetarian. I don't eat meat," she quietly remarked.

His eyes narrowed and darkened. "You don't eat meat? You've always been so difficult," he hissed.

He rushed over to the roasted pig and violently reached inside its gaping mouth; he freed the crimson apple inside. In doing so, a large chunk of flesh came off along with it. Holding the fruit in his left hand, he used his right hand to grab the animal's head from its shoulders. He tossed it violently across the room. It skidded against the floor with a greasy thud. He moved wildly over to Katie's chair and slammed the apple onto her plate.

"Would this be satisfactory?" he asked angrily.

She looked down at her apple and was immediately horrified by it. Pieces of bloody meat remained on its shiny surface. A thick tearing sound could be heard underneath its skin. The orb appeared to be pulsing, like a heartbeat. One unbelievably plump larva burst forth burst forth from the glistening skin and fell on the plate. It wiggled violently over the smooth surface. Her body went cold at the realization. Quickly she gathered her wits and tried her best to appease him.

"James, you must forgive me, you see," she hesitated, her voice shaking slightly, "I'm a little nervous about our wedding night."

She looked up innocently and tried her best to smile. Slowly the anger melted from his face. His eyes took on a softer quality.

"Oh, of course, my poor thing. Of course you are."

He sat down in a chair next to her and moved closer until they were facing one another. Taking her hands in both of his, he patted them gently. They were hot and damp. She tried her best to hide her revulsion.

"Everything is going to be just fine," he laughed softly. "In fact, I have just the thing to ease your nerves."

He reached inside his vest pocket and retrieved a small, silver flask. The ornate design was familiar. It was the same antique she remembered from her dreams. He took a wine goblet from her place setting and poured a generous portion into her glass. The pungent aroma of whiskey filled her nostrils.

"Here, my love. Cheers to my lovely bride!"

He lifted the flask for a toast. She hesitated for just a moment. This man, if that was what he was, fluttered from one emotion to the next. She was unsure of what would set off his temper. The thought of drinking something his lips touched was unsettling, though she dared not risk angering him again.

"Cheers," she said quietly.

She lifted the glass to her lips. The intoxicating aroma was bitter. She sipped the dark liquid. The taste was putrid and warm from resting in his pocket. It rolled down her throat like heavy syrup and burned as it went. Its effect was immediate. Her mind became foggy and her composure was lost. His smile widened as he realized the effect the whiskey was having on her. He stood up suddenly, taking her by the hand.

"Come, it's time for you to get dressed."

As she rose to her feet, her head swam in confusion. She had to reach for his arm to prevent from falling to the ground. He quickly steadied her by placing his arm around her waist. Together, they walked to the curtained changing area. He made his way back to the table to retrieve the dress. He carried it back to the vanity.

"Take your time, dear. I'll be waiting." His eyes were full of anticipation and excitement.

Katie tried her best to concentrate on the task at hand. She needed to stall him for as long as possible so she could come up with a plan of escape. Her mind was foggy from the whiskey. She fought the urge to lie down and sleep. She couldn't lose consciousness. It was difficult to regain her composure. She finally managed to pull the ivory dress from the box. The beauty of it took her breath away despite the circumstances. A flood of memories filled her mind and heart as she handled the gown. She was able to finally pull it over her head. For one terrifying moment, she could not breathe as the heavy satin covered her face. She struggled to pull it down further over her head finally pulling the material down around her petite figure.

Her hands would not obey as she reached behind her back to tie up the laces. There was no way she could cinch it up in the back. The realization hit her that James was the only one that could help her in this moment. The thought filled her with dread and fear. Surely, he realized this when he gave her the dress. Clutching the front with her left hand to keep her modesty, she called out to him, "James, I'm afraid I can't tie up the back of the gown."

"Oh my dear, this sounds like a job for your husband I imagine," he chuckled quietly to himself.

He entered the vanity. She made sure not to make eye contact. Slowly, he walked up behind her. She could see his reflection in the vanity mirror. His eyes were full of desire as he gazed at her bare back. She held tightly to the front of her bodice fearing what he might do next. His breath was hot against the back of her neck. To her surprise, he gently drew the back of her gown and slowly cinched it up. She could feel the tips of his fingers grazing across her shoulders. They were unusually hot and smoldering. He took his time and seemed to be enjoying her vulnerability. When he finally was finished, he carefully turned her around to face him.

"Do not be afraid, my love. I will not hurt you, as long as you are a good and obedient wife." His face grew serious as he looked into her eyes.

"Of course, James." She slowly regained her composure and tried her best to appease him.

He led her out to the main hall.

"I'm afraid that under these circumstances, we can't have a priest do the honors," he laughed darkly.

His voice was grave as he spoke the word *priest.* The sound gave her chills.

"I thought we could make do and simply say our own vows. After all, this is a new age, is it not? No sense in sticking to old customs," he added.

Katie's mind raced as she began plotting escape. The logs in the fireplace crackled as an idea began to form.

"James, I don't want to be a bother, but I am a bit cold. Would you mind stoking the fire before we lose the flames?"

"Is my lady cold? Of course, let me take care of that at once."

In his eagerness to appease her, he turned his back and set to turn the logs. For one brief moment, she was filled with a sense of pity for the man. There was an element of kindness resonating from his soul. Yet, it seemed burdened with a dark and powerful force. She wondered briefly when and where he had finally succumbed to its power. As he concentrated on the task at hand, Katie spun into action. Acting on primal instinct, she reached above the fireplace and grabbled one of the pewter candleholders on the mantel. Taking the large object in both hands, she slammed it hard against the back of his head. He fell to the floor in a motionless heap in front of the fire. She turned and ran. Her dress dragged on the cold, stone floors of the ballroom. The fabric made a strange scratching sound as it trailed the ground. She made it to the set of large antique doors. For one horrifying moment, they appeared to be locked. She pulled and pushed until they finally opened.

The enormous brass door groaned loudly on its hinges as she barely squeezed through it. The door slammed shut behind her. The physical activities made her head spin as the whiskey played havoc with her senses. The sound of her bare feet pattered softly across the cold floors. Ancient paintings of the castle's previous owners lined the dark hallway. The eyes of the portraits' subjects seemed to follow her as she made her way down the seemingly endless corridor. The candlelight cast eerie shadows over the walls. And where was her beloved Daniel during all of this? Did he have any idea where she was? If she could just manage to find her way outside the castle, she might somehow come up with a plan of rescue. She ran as fast as she could through the dark, meandering passages. Cold air painfully filled her lungs as she made her way through the ancient building. Hidden deep within the darkness and candlelight, she began to feel like an apparition, lost with the antiquity and history of the old ruin. Howling winds and rains raged outside the castle walls. The deep alcoves of stained glass took the brunt of the storm's punishment. The heavy windows shook and withstood the abuse in spite of its intensity and power. Underneath the untamed sounds of nature were raw, primitive whispers that begged to be released. The faint sounds echoed inside the decrepit walls.

The castle had its share of ghosts and spirits, each of which was determined to have their voices heard. A loud explosion of thunder erupted overhead. This was followed by a lightening strike, which lit up the night sky.

The long corridor seemed to lead to a familiar place. Fragmented memories from her childhood filled her mind. She could see herself as a young girl, sitting on a fancy, velvet chair, holding a small doll within her tiny hands. The child waited for her father to return from helping the owners with their renovation project. An occasional worker would smile and nod at her as they went about their business. A large parlor was located in the West Wing. Once inside, one had to merely walk down a short hallway, which led to the front doors of the castle. The memory faded and she realized with complete certainty that this was her one chance at escaping. A glimmer of hope began to surface in her heart. The passageway should lead her to the main entryway. She came to a stop at the end of the corridor.

With eager anticipation, she pushed against the heavy brass doors and made her way into the dimly lit space. A large fireplace roared with bright flames. The warmth was a welcoming sensation. With tentative steps, she made her way inside, where it soon became apparent this was not the parlor of her childhood. To her dismay, she found herself inside a large bedroom. Realizing this, she stopped.

A faint whisper began to emanate.

"Katie, where are you?" She realized it was the voice of Daniel.

Her heart began to beat in anticipation. The sound seemed to be coming from the far wall of the bedroom. The wind and rain continued raging outside the castle's walls. She called out loudly, trying desperately to make her voice heard in the roaring storm.

"Daniel, I'm inside Dunguaire Castle. I'm trying to find my way to the West Wing, but I'm lost."

In spite of her fear, she found herself walking toward the fireplace to warm her body. Her eyes adjusted to the dark, candlelit room and wandered over the lavish décor. Crystal vases containing brilliant pink roses filled the space. A large canopy bed was placed across from the fireplace. Hundreds of rose petals covered the velvet bedspread. Candles were set throughout the room giving it an air of romance. Her heart began to race, as a tightening sensation filled her throat. Her eyes slowly lifted, taking in an enormous wall painting above the fireplace mantel. To her dismay, she recognized the portrait's subject all too well.

The oil painting depicted Katie in her wedding dress, staring out into space, completely lost in the void. Her eyes were hollow and resonated shock and apathy. Her fair skin was ghostly white, sickly, and translucent. Blood red lips appeared cold and unnatural. She knew at once that this was to be her future with James if she stayed.

Strange music began surfacing at the top of the mantel. She realized that it was coming from a familiar tin box. The handle turned on its own in a slow and methodic rhythm. In spite of what was happening around her, she seemed locked into place unable to move. A shrill voice began to sing in a high pitch melody.

My mother taught me how to sew,

And how to thread the needle,

Every time my finger slips,

Pop! goes the weasel.

You may try to sew and sew,

And never make something regal,

So roll it up and let it go,

Pop! goes the weasel.

The music sped up, ascending in volume until it threatened to destroy her mind.

I went a'hunting in the woods,

It wasn't very legal.

The dog and I were caught with the goods,

Pop! goes the weasel.

I said I didn't hunt or sport,

The warden looked at my beagle,

He said to tell it to the court,

Pop! goes the weasel.

The box opened on the last verse as a gust of cold wind blew back her hair. A dark, obscured image of an elderly woman emerged and hovered above. Where her eyes should have been were dark, empty sockets. The apparition began to moan and scream. It's keening filled the room with its agonizing wail. The Banshee's distorted mouth stretched unbelievably wide. Katie covered her ears in an attempt to escape the maddening cries. Her mind felt as if it would split from the anguished howls. Everything in her being told her to run, to get out of the room, and yet her body would not obey. Without warning, the ghostly phantom disappeared back into the box. Sadly, this relief was short-lived.

CHAPTER 32

No one has greater love than this, to lay down one's life for one's friends.

- John, 15:13, Saint Joseph Edition of The New American Bible

Heavy footsteps echoed in the dark hallway. Her body could not break its paralysis. In a cold daze, she was only partially aware of the rough hands grabbing at the back of her shoulders, turning her around. James stood in front of her with blood rushing down his face from the wound she had inflicted.

"So, you found our bridal suite. After all that I have done for you. You repay me with yet another betrayal. You little whore! Mark my words. You will not betray me again!"

A blind rage washed over his pallid face as he spoke. "You are going to learn a lesson tonight that you will never forget."

His dark eyes turned scarlet red as his skin pulsed and rippled. He grabbed her by the wrists and shoved her to the ground in front of the fireplace. His pale body distorted and began to elongate. His legs lengthened grotesquely before him. The tailored trousers split open. Dark, wiry hair sprouted like putrid moss on his pulsing legs. His flesh bubbled underneath the tattered remnants of cloth. The translucent skin split and tore across his skull and face. Clots of bloody, blond hair fell to the ground in a meaty pile. He stood over her menacingly in the firelight.

"Let me go!" Katie moaned.

James replied in a dark, demonic voice, "I will never let you go. Katie, from this night forward, you belong to me. There will be no more delays. No more distractions. Your games have come to an end. Let our wedding night commence," he laughed insanely.

He pushed her down onto the cold, stone floor. His death-like stench awoke her from her paralysis. She screamed and scratched at his face with renewed strength and determination. As she made contact with his flesh, there was a sickening sensation of skin peeling off under her fingernails. Underneath was an oozing, dark mass of pulsing muscle. She struggled wildly as her nightmare became a reality.

As her body slowly began to lose strength, and her spirit begged for mercy from this undeniably gruesome fate, the room suddenly exploded with a burst of magnificent light and sound. At first, she believed the noise to be that of the lightening and thunder sounding outside the castle windows. Her eye s stared in shock and happiness as Daniel stood above the demon. His beautiful ebony wings filled the room with a dazzling spectrum of white light. In his right hand was a large silver sword that glowed brilliantly in the darkness.

"Let go of her, demon!" he called in a powerful voice.

The creature released Katie and quickly stood. The two faced one other silently. After a moment, James began to speak.

"Oh, this is quite the reunion isn't it?" he spat in a thick, demonic voice.

His body towered over Katie in a threatening fashion. A grin emerged on his misshapen face. Razor sharp teeth clashed with a nauseous grinding sound as he spoke.

"So you came back for another round. Wasn't once enough for you? I'm losing my patience, angel. You've interrupted our wedding night," he growled ominously.

"In the Name of the Father, the Son, and the Holy Spirit. Go back to the Hell you came from!" Daniel commanded.

James hissed menacingly as he spoke, "Have you forgotten where you are? You have no power here," he laughed cruelly.

Katie began to realize that something was very wrong. Daniel's face was shadowed with sorrow.

"You are too late," James laughed looking around the bedroom. "This is our special love nest. Isn't it romantic?" he hissed. "She can never leave and there is no going back now. The rules have changed, angel. The game is over." His grin widened into a menacing sneer.

Daniel studied James for a moment. In an instant, he was in the air with his powerful wings outstretched. He lowered the sword down onto the demon's pulsing neck. The creature moved away moments before being struck. He rose into the air facing Daniel.

"Can't you do better than that?" he mocked.

It stretched its claws toward his chest.

"I want to see that big heart of yours."

He lunged forward. The sharp talons grazed the front of Daniel's shirt ripping the cloth and tearing brutally across his skin. Crimson streaks began spreading outward on his chest. Daniel flew backwards in pain. The demon followed. The two opponents levitated toward the high ceiling. Katie watched in horror as they took turns striking blows at one another. Eventually their movements appeared like a blurry mist as they battled with supernatural speed. Daniel swung his sword once again making contact with the demon's neck. A stream of black gore flowed from the wound like thick syrup and bubbled down his throat. The demon clutched his neck and grimaced. A cloud of smoke steamed from the cut. As the nauseating fumes permeated the room, he fell backward lowering his hands. In an instant, the deadly injury healed itself and the wound quickly sealed over.

"You can't really hurt me, Daniel," he laughed.

The creature lunged forward until their faces were inches apart. James grinned at him mockingly. Daniel switched his sword to his left hand and punched him squarely in the face. The demon let out an angry howl, lost his balance, and fell down toward the floor. He landed next to Katie on the cold stones. Without warning, he lunged toward her, grabbing her arm; he pulled her tightly against his hot body. She winced and tried to pull away. Her eyes burned and watered from the terrible aroma of sulfur and rotting flesh. His long claws pressed against her throat.

"Let her go!" Daniel demanded.

"Would you like to watch her bleed?" His claws tightened around her throat.

Small beads of blood rose to the surface of her skin. Searing pain burned into her flesh. Katie screamed as he pierced her delicate skin. Daniel, alarmed, demanded, "Let her go!"

"Put down your sword, angel. I will kill her in front of you if you do not."

Anger washed over Daniels face. He dropped his sword to the floor. The sharp clanging sound of polished steel reverberated throughout the castle.

"That's better. You see, Katie, even Daniel can learn to obey. It's not that difficult now is it?"

"Please James, let him leave. I will stay. Please don't hurt him."

She could feel his hot flesh moving and pulsing against her body.

"Isn't that nice. You need to shut your mouth or I will permanently close it!" He traced one razor sharp claw in front of her lips. "Do you understand me?" Katie nodded.

Holding her tightly in his left arm, the demonic creature reached down and took up the sword in his right hand.

"Well isn't that a big one?" he said, between bursts of laugher. "Get down on your knees and face the fire. Be a good lad and obey me."

Slowly and carefully Daniel lowered to the floor. He gazed out at the fire with his chin set and face determined. Tears streamed down Katie's face. Her body began shaking violently and she feared for his life.

"Please, James," she whispered, "I will do anything you want. Please let him go. I'm begging you."

"Oh yes, darling, you will do what I say. It's not a question." As he spoke, his voice changed back and forth from human to a thick, demonic tone.

With one sharp motion, he brought the sword down on Daniel's back and shoulders. The razor sharp blade tore into his right wing. Daniel screamed in agony as the sword cut through his flesh.

"No!!!!" Katie screamed. "God have mercy!!! Daniel!!!!!"

He writhed on the floor, clenching in a fetal position from the intense pain. The demon roared with laughter at his work. In his glee, he loosened his grip on Katie. She took the opportunity to brake away. She rushed to Daniel's side and fell next to him. Gently, she lifted his head into her lap. A dark pool of blood began forming around him as the scarlet wound gushed out on the cold stone.

"Daniel, no, please, no. Stay with me!" She wept loudly as tears poured down over his handsome face.

Daniel stared up into her eyes and looked at her sadly.

"I am so sorry, my love." His jaw clenched painfully in a tight grimace.

Katie could feel the life force drifting away from him. The sharp sound of the demon's hooves dragged across the floor as he drew closer.

"Stand back, Katie. I need to even up my work on the other side," he smiled cruelly.

"Leave him alone!"

"Stand there if you like, my love, it's all the same to me," he laughed.

The demon towered over them. He raised the sword high in the air. The gleaming steel shone brightly in the reflection of the candlelight. Daniel slowly and painfully pushed himself onto his elbow and turned to face the creature. With one fluid motion, he reached into his vest pocket and retrieved the pewter Crucifix. His eyes glowed with renewed determination as he held the beloved cross.

In a loud voice he cried, "In the Name of Jesus Christ, I cast you back to Hell, demon!" He propelled the Crucifix and it struck James fully in the chest. He shrieked in pain and surprise as the metal burned into his flesh.

Steam and vapors exploded from his body. James fell onto the floor writhing in agony. Collapsing into a fit of seizures, his demonic form changed and dissolved. His body gradually turned back to human shape. He crawled across the floor toward Katie. His pale face was pained and sorrowful. Tears fell from his eyes and his mouth trembled. With a weak voice he cried out, "Katie, please forgive me. I did it all for you, my love."

She was overwhelmed with shock and confusion by what had just transpired. In spite of what had taken place, there was a part of her that understood that James had been possessed. He had surrendered himself to evil. Her heart was filled with pity for the dying man.

"I am not the one you should be asking forgiveness of," she said sadly.

His eyes filled with sorrowful regret. He looked up mournfully and prayed, "Please God forgive me. I have greatly sinned. Lord have mercy." His eyes closed slowly as his spirit departed.

Katie turned her attention back to Daniel. A slight smile covered his faced as he gazed up lovingly.

"My love, you're safe. I love you so much, my Katie girl." His beautiful blue eyes closed softly. As he took his last breath, a peaceful glow washed over him.

"Daniel. Oh no, Daniel!" She kissed him gently as her tears streamed down her face.

Overcome with grief, she closed her eyes and wept over his body. The room suddenly began to spin and to lose focus and she was transported back to her cabin.

CHAPTER 33

To Love another person is to see the face of God.

-Victor Hugo, Les Misérables

In a state of shock, she found herself on her bedroom floor. The ceiling had splintered above the bed. Large chunks of wood and varnish had fallen down on the comforter. She slowly stood up realizing shards of glass covered the floor. The cold night air whipped through her bedroom curtains. The picture window was completely shattered.

Her body was ice cold as she made her way to the front door of the cabin. Bright lights flickered outside the kitchen windows. She managed to walk to the front porch. Several police cruisers were parked in her driveway. The lights hurt her eyes. The officers called out loudly to her:

"Are you Katie O'Brien?"

"Yes?" she answered in a daze.

"Your security system has reported a possible break in."

She continued to stare out at the police officers. Out of the group of men appeared a single female patrol officer. She was tall and slender with short blond hair and a compassionate face.

"Ms. O'Brien, would you like to sit in my car while the officers look inside your house?" she asked kindly.

"Yes." Katie answered in a faraway voice. "That would be fine."

They headed over to the police cruiser and sat down in the back seat.

Once inside, she began answering a series of questions regarding the proposed break in. Her mind wandered as she tried to explain the fact that she had awoken to the damage in her bedroom and the sound of the security alarm going off. Even in a state of shock, Katie realized that telling them the truth would most likely result in a trip to the psych ward. After answering the officer's questions, Sergeant McShane asked if she would like to contact her family or friends.

"Yes," she whispered, "I would like to call my neighbors."

About fifteen minutes later, Camellia and Steven arrived at the cabin. Mercifully, the house alarm had been turned off as well as the police sirens. Frogs and crickets had replaced the manmade sounds with their natural ballad. They parked their van next to the patrol cars and hurried over to see their friend.

"Are you alright, Katie?" Camellia asked frantically.

It was impossible to explain what had just happened.

"I…" she hesitated, "My bedroom window is broken, I don't know what happened."

Steven looked at her with concern.

"I think she's in shock, Camellia. Katie, we want you to come home with us tonight."

She looked up and nodded absently. The police officers took turns questioning her, inspecting the cabin, and dusting for fingerprints. It seemed to go on forever before they'd finished. The cruisers finally drove away. Afterwards, the Sanchez's led Katie back to the cabin. It seemed contaminated in the wake of the violence, and the recent police investigation.

"Honey, lets go to your bedroom and get you a nice overnight bag ready," Camellia suggested.

Katie nodded mechanically. Broken glass crushed under their feet as they made their way into the bedroom.

"Katie, I know a wonderful cleaning woman that can help you with this mess."

"Thank you," she answered absently.

Camellia was worried by her friend's unusual behavior. She seemed to be in a trance as she gathered her items together.

"Do you need a coat or sweater? It's pretty chilly tonight."

In a daze, she pulled a jean jacket from her closet. She draped it over her shoulders and they left arm and arm for the van. Just as her hand reached the handle, Katie looked up in alarm as she remembered her friend's son.

"Camellia, is Bennie alright?"

"Yes. Why do you ask?"

She took a deep breath of relief and replied, "I had the strangest dream about him tonight."

"Don't worry," Camellia gently assured her. "Lizzie is back at the house taking care of the children.

"I was just wondering if he was safe…."

When they arrived back at the Sanchez home, Camellia led Katie to the guest bedroom and helped her get settled. She sensed her need for privacy and did not linger too long.

"Let me know if there is anything you need tonight. Our room is just down the hall on the right.

"Thank you," Katie answered absently.

She solemnly finished unpacking her overnight bag and brought her toiletries to the bathroom. She changed into a pair of soft flannel pajamas and climbed into the comfortable full size bed. The room was decorated with a combination of burgundy and cream accents. A painting of a vineyard rested above the bed. A large, golden Crucifix hung over the oak dresser across the room. Looking at the cross gave her a sense of peace in spite of the horrors that she had just endured. She climbed into bed and drifted immediately to sleep.

The next morning, Katie awoke to the sounds of excited children preparing for their school day. She took a quick shower and dressed in the guest bathroom. Her outfit consisted of an old pair of jeans, a long sleeve flannel shirt covered with a jean jacket.

Her skin was still cold to the touch even after the warm shower and extra layers of clothing. She slipped into a pair of white Keds and headed to the kitchen. The family was sitting around the table eating breakfast. There were plates of pancakes and scrambled eggs surrounded by pitchers of milk and orange juice. The children beamed at her excitedly.

"Hi Katie!" they all waved happily in unison.

Their parents had not explained the reason of her overnight visit. The children believed that she was simply enjoying a fun sleepover at their house.

Katie held her overnight bag on her arm. Bennie grinned up at her. She returned the smile, grateful that he was safe.

"Good morning, Katie. Come on over and join us for breakfast. I can make fresh pancakes if you like," Camellia encouraged.

"Thank you. If you don't mind, I'm going to walk down the hill and go back to my cabin. I have some things to sort out," she answered in monotone.

Camellia and Steven exchanged worried looks.

"Katie, I hope you don't mind, but I called a window repair service, one that I use in my contracting jobs. They're planning to come by this afternoon and repair your bedroom window," Steven gently remarked. "We would be more than happy to give you a ride if you'd like," he added.

Katie looked up and thanked him for his thoughtfulness. "It's kind of you…but the exercise would do me good." The family reluctantly agreed.

"Katie, when you're ready for an outing, I'd love to take you out for coffee," Camellia replied.

"That'd be nice," she smiled.

Bennie suddenly jumped up out of his chair and hugged her. "Don't worry, Katie. You're going to be just fine," he announced confidently.

She hugged him back and as she did this hot tears rose in her eyes. She couldn't imagine her life ever being the same after that night. Her heart felt like it had been ripped out of her chest leaving behind an empty husk in its place. She put on a brave face for the benefit of the family and said her goodbyes, pulling her overnight bag over her shoulder as she made her way out the door.

The air was clean from last night's storm. The hazy sunlight reflected the dew covering the shrubbery lining the borders of the walkway. She slowly made her way down toward the dirt-covered trail that led to her cabin. A loud rustling shook the foliage following the curve of the road. The noise made her jump in her tracks. Out of the thicket emerged a tall, young buck. The antlers were impressively large on his head. The animal stood his ground for a moment before crossing the road. The eyes of the creature were a deep mahogany brown and startling in their awareness. He slowly crossed the dirt path, turning briefly to look back at Katie before trotting back into the dense woods. The strange encounter did not faze her in the least. She continued to make her way down the hill lost in her thoughts.

Time escaped her. Eventually she found herself standing in front of her cabin. She could see the remnants of the yellow security tape running to the back of the house. The police had failed to clean up after their investigation. She knew she would be busy trying to get the house back in order. She wandered up the porch steps and reached for the front door. Her hand held the porcelain knob but couldn't seem to find the motivation to turn it. Instead, she walked over to the porch swing and sat down. She dropped her tote bag by her feet. Looking out at the woods left her feeling empty and alone.

The sharp aroma of the grand oak trees filled her senses. The mid morning sun gently caressed the moist, forested canopy. Steam rose from the rain-soaked flora. The natural beauty of the forest would have normally filled her heart and mind with happiness and peace, and yet on this sad morning she observed the miraculous scenery with a numb indifference. An empty void had replaced her newly awakened heart and soul. In its place, a feeling of hopelessness had taken refuge. She took a deep, anguished sigh and leaned back against her wooden porch swing.

Her solitude was interrupted by a loud honking sound coming from the side of her house. Cozy The Goose waddled up to the porch. His white plumage shone brilliantly in the early morning sun. His sparkling eyes glowed in excitement as he discovered Katie sitting on her porch swing. Relief washed over her as she realized that her gentle goose was safe after last night.

"Hello, sweet thing," she tiredly whispered.

He honked happily in response and carefully hopped up the porch steps. To her surprise, he made his way over to her feet gently resting his face against her white tennis shoes. She reached down and stroked his downy head. He closed his bright, velvety eyes at her touch.

A sense of peace came with the knowledge that her little friend was unharmed. Katie closed her eyes and surrendered to the sounds of the forest. The melodic calls of the songbirds sang out softy among the impressive collection of trees. The amphibious inhabitants of the lake joined in the harmonies. These soothing sounds flowed over one another for several minutes. Unexpectedly, they were interrupted by a loud rustling noise directly behind her cabin. Katie reluctantly opened her eyes, expecting another deer or wild animal making its way out from the thicket of vines and brush.

But this was not the case. Instead, there appeared to be a man emerging from the protection of the woods. Alarmed, Katie sat up in surprise and fear at the unexpected intruder. The stranger surfaced from the tangled collection of honeysuckle vines. Shadowed at first from the dense foliage, his form slowly became evident in the soft morning light. Dark auburn highlights shone beautifully on his thick, wavy hair. The handsome man's vivid blue eyes gazed intently at his beloved. Daniel stopped several yards away and smiled down at Katie's shocked and startled face. Her mind could not grasp what she was seeing. She did not dare believe this. It simply couldn't be.

With long strides, he quickly closed the distance between them. Standing before her, just a few feet away, he slowly took off his hat, looked her squarely in the eyes, and asked, "May I sit there beside you, my love?"

She stared in disbelief. "Daniel?"

"Yes, Katie, your eyes are not deceiving you."

He carefully sat down next to her on the swing. He looked at her kindly and gently took her hand kissing it softly. His lips were warm and sensual on her cold skin. Her heart flooded in search of a rational explanation for his being there.

"I thought I'd lost you," she whispered in a shaking voice.

"I've been given another chance. It turns out that you do sometimes get a second try in life," he smiled brightly looking deeply into her eyes.

"Oh Daniel."

He reached down gently, taking her face in his hands; he kissed her softly.

"This is real. I'm not dreaming?" she asked desperately.

"Yes, my love, this is real."

They held each other tightly for what seemed like a small eternity. Katie's heart slowly regained its steady beat. Her body warmed to his touch.

Daniel quietly lowered himself to the ground and retrieved a green, velvet box. "Katie, would you please do me the honor of being my wife?"

Tears flowed down her face.

"Oh yes, Daniel, my beloved."

He took her left hand and carefully slipped the antique diamond ring onto her finger. It fit as perfectly as it had so many years before.

"You've made me the happiest man on earth, my Katie girl! Oh, and one more thing, my love. Would you wear this golden locket?"

She smiled excitedly, admiring his beautiful face.

"Where did you find it?" she asked.

He gave her a quick wink and slipped the chain delicately around her neck. The locket fell against her heart. The sensation was absolutely exquisite. They both stood up and embraced passionately. Daniel slipped his arms around the small of her back and pulled her closer. Her hands eagerly explored his strong arms and chest. She pulled away, surprised by what was missing behind his broad shoulders.

"Sorry, my love, I traded in my wings for an earthbound life. I hope you don't mind?"

"Of course not," she sighed. "All I want is for the rest of our lives to be normal."

The both laughed as they held each other passionately.

In their moment of bliss, they failed to hear the vehicle moving up the driveway. An explosion of children's laughter could be heard coming from the open window of the van. The two lovers stepped away from each other. Camellia and Steven were grinning inside. The entire family quickly made their way out of the van and stood staring with curious expressions. Camellia beamed happily and said,

"Sorry to interrupt. We were just worried about you making it home and thought we'd stop by."

Katie blushed. "Oh, I want you to meet my fiancé, Daniel McCarthy," she smiled back.

Steven and Camellia exchanged a look. Camellia was the first to break the awkward silence.

"Mi amiga! I'm so happy for you!" She wrapped her arms around Katie and gave her a big hug, in her ear she quietly whispered, "He's so handsome!"

Camellia smiled excitedly. Steven reached out to shake Daniel's hand. The two men introduced one another and seemed to hit it off immediately. Camellia's eyes looked down at Katie's engagement ring.

"It's gorgeous!" she exclaimed.

The children began giggling behind their parents. Lizzie was all smiles, admiring Daniel. She made eye contact and gave a quick thumbs up. Katie smiled back happily. Camellia clapped her hands together with excitement.

"It looks like we have a wedding to plan! We have flower girls and ring bearer if you are looking for volunteers."

The children squealed excitedly in response.

"Camellia, would you be my matron of honor?" Katie asked.

"Of course I will!" Camellia answered excitedly.

Camellia turned to Daniel and asked if he had a best man in mind.

"I'm afraid that I am pretty far from home. I do not, my lady."

Steven interrupted, "I would be happy to volunteer as your best man. Katie is a member of our family now. This means that you will be part of it as well."

Daniel reached out to shake Steven's hand. "It would be an honor, sir."

Camellia smiled in response to his thick, Celtic brogue. "Is that an Irish accent, Daniel?"

"Yes it is, my lady," Daniel answered politely. "I'm from a small village in Galway by the name of Kinvara. I don't suppose you've heard of it?"

She paused for a moment, and tried to remember why the name sounded so familiar. In a moment of shocked disbelief, Camellia quickly glanced between Katie and Daniel. "I've heard of the town of Kinvara," she answered quietly. "Katie mentioned the same town to me awhile back."

Camellia locked eyes with her friend and begged the silent question. Steven looked at his wife unsure of why Daniel's Irish background was so startling. He interrupted by turning the conversation back to the subject of the wedding.

"It's settled then. I'm sure Father Peter will be happy to bless your marriage," he smiled.

The family chatted about the upcoming wedding and made a dinner date for the following Sunday. Camellia quickly grabbed Katie by her hand and hugged her tightly. She bent down and whispered in her ear, "I will be calling you up for a private coffee tomorrow! I have so many questions."

"I can't wait to tell you all about it, Camellia. It's quite the tale," Katie whispered back.

The family said their goodbyes as they made their way back into the van. They slowly headed down the driveway, and onto their way to school.

Hand in hand, the two lovers walked back to the cabin in the woods. They happily sat down together on the old porch swing, where Katie rested her head against Daniel's strong shoulder. Gently, he pushed back the auburn curls from her forehead.

"Any ideas for our honeymoon, my love?" Daniel asked softly. Katie smiled up at him.

"Anywhere I am safe in your arms will be absolutely perfect," she sighed.

His dark blue eyes widened as he said, "I think Holland's a good place to start. I'm long overdue for getting you a pair of wooden shoes for your pretty feet," he grinned.

His beautiful smile brought the dimples out onto his face. They looked at one other lovingly and laughed happily together.

"Now don't forget, my love, I promised you a ride on the back of a zebra. Do you recall?"

"I do," Katie smiled brightly at the memory.

He gazed into her eyes and drew her close. He kissed her with an unbridled desire, tracing his fingers down the hollow of her neck, stopping momentarily to touch the golden locket hanging between her breasts. His lips followed where his hands caressed. The sensation sent chills down the base of her spine. She was utterly lost, and in love. Drawing her even closer, Daniel whispered passionately against her soft lips, "They say the sunsets in Africa will take your breath away...."

The End

www.ingramcontent.com/pod-product-compliance
Lightning Source LLC
Chambersburg PA
CBHW021054130626
46552CB00005B/2094